WHODUNNIT DIDN'T DO IT

Edited by
Dean Wesley Smith

I0602741

Stories from Pulphouse
FICTION MAGAZINE

PUBLISHING

Whodunnit Didn't Do It

Published by WMG Publishing Inc.
All stories reprinted from the pages of
Pulphouse Fiction Magazine
Cover and interior design copyright © 2024 WMG Publishing, Inc.
Cover art copyright © by sarah5 | Depositphotos

ISBN-13 (trade paperback): 978-1-56146-996-3

MORE FROM PULPHOUSE

PULPHOUSE FICTION MAGAZINE **SUBSCRIPTION**

Available in eBook and Paper subscriptions

Go to **www.pulphousemagazine.com**

- 6 Monthly Issues in eBook
- 6 Monthly Issues in Trade Paperback
- 12 Monthly Issues in eBook
- 12 Montly Issues in Trade Paperback

PREVIOUS PULPHOUSE ISSUES

Go to www.pulphousemagazine.com to buy any of our previous issues, including the very first Issue Zero!

MORE STORIES FROM *PULPHOUSE FICTION MAGAZINE*

A Twist of a Knife

Alibi Murder

Aliens Among Us

Cattitude Edited

Destination Tomorrow or Yesterday

Don't Touch My Magic!

Ghosts Among Us

History Repeats for No Reason

Implode the Membrane

Jingle My Bells

No Way: Totally Twisted Tales

Run!! Creatures, Critters, and Pulphousers...

Snot-Nosed Aliens

That's Really Messed Up

There'll Be Blue Popcorn Without You!

Three Sheets to the Wind

Twisted Robots, Oh, My!

STORIES FROM THE ORIGINAL PULPHOUSE

Stories from the Original Pulphouse: A Fiction Magazine

Stories from Pulphouse: The Hardback Magazine

ALSO BY
DEAN WESLEY SMITH

COLD POKER GANG

Kill Game

Cold Call

Calling Dead

Bad Beat

Dead Hand

Freezeout

Ace High

Burn Card

Heads Up

Ring Game

Bottom Pair

Case Card

THE POKER BOY UNIVERSE

POKER BOY

The Slots of Saturn: A Poker Boy Novel

They're Back: A Poker Boy Short Novel

Luck Be Ladies: A Poker Boy Collection

Playing a Hunch: A Poker Boy Collection

A Poker Boy Christmas: A Poker Boy Collection

Dry Creek Crossing

Hot Springs Meadow

Green Valley

SEEDERS UNIVERSE

Dust and Kisses: A Seeders Universe Prequel Novel

Against Time

Sector Justice

Morning Song

The High Edge

Star Mist

Star Rain

Star Fall

Starburst

Rescue Two

CONTENTS

WHODUNNIT DIDN'T DO IT

INTRODUCTION

DEAN WESLEY SMITH

This was a really fun anthology to put together. Mystery/Crime. That's what the title sort of implied.

As anyone who reads *Pulphouse Fiction Magazine* knows, I love mystery stories of all kinds, and especially when the mystery happens in a fantasy or science fiction setting. Those really catch my attention as an editor.

Also, almost every issue I have a wonderful detective story from O'Neil De Noux, maybe the best writer of detective fiction working right now.

And I also get lucky and get great mystery or crime stories from Kristine Kathryn Rusch and David H. Hendrickson, both award-winning mystery and crime writers.

They also write award-winning science fiction and fantasy and everything else, but I always love the crime stories they send my way.

And in this issue I also have a story from Christina F. York who is a well-known cozy mystery writer under different pen names. Her story in this anthology is not a cozy by a long ways.

So putting this together only got hard when I decided I would not use any story from any of the other nineteen anthologies of *Pulphouse Fiction Magazine* stories that came before.

Now that made it challenging. But still fun because I got to go back and look at a lot of stories. In thirty issues, we have published around 500 stories so far, and more every month now.

That's a lot of issues and a lot of stories to look back through. Fantastic fun.

I sure hope you enjoy reading these stories as much as I did putting this together.

Dean Wesley Smith
Las Vegas, NV

LIVE THE PULPHOUSE LIFE!

Grab your Pulphouse mug and fill it with your favorite beverage and lounge in your coziest chair with the Thumper pillow while you read the latest issue of *Pulphouse*.

Want to mark off the date when your next issue will arrive? Get the *Pulphouse* calendar featuring some of our favorite *Pulphouse* cartoons!

Find all this and so much more at the *Pulphouse Fiction Magazine* online store at:

http://pulphousemagazine.com

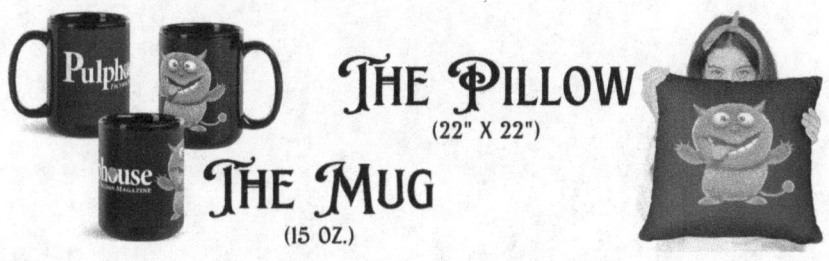

And say hi to Thumper while you're there.

FORT DUMPSTER
O'NEIL DE NOUX

O'Neil De Noux might be the best short story writer of detective fiction working today. I say something like that that every time, with every one of his stories, because it's true. And I just can't think of a better way to describe O'Neil's incredible talent at taking us into his worlds. And yes, I have said that before as well.

O'Neil has published almost fifty novels with more coming regularly. His awards include The United Kingdom Short Story Prize, the Shamus Award (for best private eye fiction), the Derringer Award (for excellence in mystery short fiction) and Police Book of the Year. Two of his stories have appeared in the prestigious Best American Mystery Stories annual anthology. You can find out a lot more about his work at his website http://www.oneildenoux.com/

FORT DUMPSTER

O'NEIL DE NOUX

March 5, 1982

Criminal District Court, New Orleans

"A single blow to the head." Detective LaStanza looked at the jury as he answered the defense attorney's question.

"Just *one* blow?" Harry Crystal said, his voice rising slightly. In his seventies, the old fox was trying his best with a bad case. LaStanza would have felt sorry for Crystal if the attorney hadn't skewered LaStanza on the witness stand on several previous cases.

Well over six-feet, Crystal was a thin man with silver hair and a slight Mississippi accent, which gave him a warm, country presentation, especially in the mini-New York called New Orleans, where most people, including LaStanza spoke with a standard-issue Orleans accent, flat *A's* and harsh vowels, sounding Brooklynese. An image of Gregory Peck as Atticus Finch came to LaStanza's mind as he watched Crystal standing behind the defense table, fiddling with a pocket watch he'd slipped from his vest.

Who the hell carried a pocket watch these days?

Crystal looked up, focusing his dark brown eyes at LaStanza and said, "Were there any knife wounds on Mr. Shoemaker's body?"

"It did not appear so, Sir."

Crystal's eyebrows rose. "Did not appear?"

LaStanza looked at the jury again. "I'm not an expert on wounds, Sir. Besides the crushed skull, there were six wounds on Mr. Shoemaker's body, two on his hands, two on his side and one on each leg. They appeared to be abrasions, but I cannot testify if they were or weren't inflicted by a knife." Looking at Crystal, he quickly added, "I'm sure the pathologist can give a more scientific explanation of the wounds."

"Detective," Judge DeSalvo cut in. "You will confine your remarks to what you know, not what the pathologist may or may not explain."

"Yes, Sir."

Crystal came right back. "Now let me get this straight. You charge my client with First Degree Murder because he allegedly attacked the victim with a knife and yet there were no knife wounds." Crystal was doing what good defense lawyers did — creating a smoke screen to mask the guilt of the accused.

"Objection," Assistant D.A. Judy Brown stood. "If counsel has a question, let him ask it." She adjusted her black horn-rimmed glasses. Judy was a petite woman with lifeless brown hair and the sharpest legal mind LaStanza knew. If Crystal was a fox, she was the ultimate fox hound.

Judge DeSalvo waved the attorneys forward. A husky man

with salt-and-pepper hair and a matching beard, DeSalvo was obviously displeased with the sparring. LaStanza looked over at the defendant. Michael Bellinger, in a blue suit, sat behind the defense table with his arms folded and stared straight ahead. He looked smaller than six-two in that ill-fitted suit. Clean-shaven, brown hair cropped short, skin a jailhouse pallor of faded pink, he seemed to have gained weight awaiting trial in parish prison. Probably the first time in years he'd had three meals a day. He wouldn't return LaStanza's stare, hadn't looked at him since the trial started.

LaStanza leaned back and ran his hand through his wavy, dark brown hair. He needed a haircut. Again. He patted his full moustache with his fingers. Olive complected with light green, Sicilian eyes, the detective stood five-six and weighed a lean one-thirty. A distance runner in high school, he carried the same weight at thirty-two. Turning to the jury, he made eye contact with a black man in a tan suit, then with a young white man in a polo shirt. Moving his gaze along the jury, he tried his best to connect with them.

When the attorneys returned to their positions, Crystal asked his next question. "Why did you charge my client with First Degree Murder?"

LaStanza wanted to explain to the jury they always charge murderers with the most serious degree as they built their case. Kept them from making bail easily and if the D.A. thought the charge should be lowered, let the D.A. lower it. But that sounded complicated, so he looked at the jury and said, "During an armed robbery ..."

"What armed robbery?" Crystal interrupted.

DeSalvo cut him off. "Counselor, let the officer finish his answer."

LaStanza lowered his normally forceful voice so the jury would have to concentrate to listen. "Michael Bellinger went after Mr. Shoemaker with a knife to rob Mr. Shoemaker, who knocked the knife away from Mr. Bellinger, who picked up a big rock and hit Mr. Shoemaker on the head. Mr. Bellinger rifled Mr. Shoemaker's clothes and took his money. Five dollars and fifty-seven cents."

"In Louisiana," Judge DeSalvo injected to the jury, "as I explained in my initial instructions to you as the trial began, a murder during the commission of certain felonies qualifies as First Degree Murder. Armed Robbery is one of those felonies. I will elaborate in your final instructions." DeSalvo looked back at Crystal. "Now let's move on."

LaStanza fanned his blue suit coat to allow some of the lame air-conditioning to cool him. A woman juror, middle-aged, with sandy hair smiled and fanned herself with a sheet of paper. LaStanza smiled slightly in response. He was connecting and that was good. They were paying attention to his testimony and hopefully would like him and believe what he said. Everyone played legal gamesmanship in court, lawyers, witnesses, even judges. Everyone wanted to win.

Crystal stood looking down at his notes for a moment, his shoulders sinking. Maybe he was feeling his age after all. He took in a breath and said, "Detective LaStanza, did you beat my client to get his confession?"

"No, Sir." LaStanza answered, turned to the jury to show he was serious.

"You never struck him at any time."

"That's correct."

"Have you ever beaten anyone to get a confession?" It was the old police brutality defense and Crystal was putting it out to give the jury something to ponder, but LaStanza was ready.

Letting his gaze move across the jury as he answered, LaStanza kept his voice firm. "No, Sir. Beating people for confessions is useless. Hell, you beat me and I'll confess to the Kennedy Assassination to get you to stop." His voice rose, "It's of no value."

Crystal's face remained stern. "Isn't it true you've been accused of police brutality seventeen times?"

LaStanza gave Judy Brown a moment to object, but she just nodded slightly to him. He wanted to tell the jury it was a common defense attorney ploy to have accused criminals file an accusation against police officers, to cloud the issue, but this wasn't the time for speeches, so he said, "I don't know how many times I've been accused, but each accusation was investigated and all have been deemed *unfounded*. Without merit."

Crystal opened his arms. "Seventeen accusations and all without merit!"

LaStanza keep his face as expressionless as he could.

Crystal waited a moment before asking, "Det. LaStanza, are you a Vietnam veteran?"

"Yes, Sir."

"What branch of the service?"

"U.S. Army."

"Ever hear of the My Lai massacre?"

"Yes, Sir."

"Were you ever involved in any massacres?"

"Objection!" Judy Brown stood. She opened her mouth to continue, just sat and said, "Never mind." A bored look on her face told the jury to let the old man ramble.

LaStanza figured Crystal would bring up Vietnam, since the accused and the victim were also Vietnam vets. Maybe he planned to paint all of them, including LaStanza, with the same brush. They were all village-burning, baby-killing Viet vets.

Crystal repeated his question about massacres.

LaStanza looked into the eyes of a black woman juror in a maroon dress as he said, "My Lai occurred in 1968. I was still in high school. Didn't go to Vietnam until 1974. The only massacre I saw was the Michelon Plantation Massacre." LaStanza turned back to Crystal. "I took pictures of the bodies of U.S. Marines executed by the Viet Cong."

Crystal bit his lower lip pensively before asking, "Det. LaStanza, how many men have you killed?"

"Objection, your honor." Judy stood, fists on her hips. "No, go ahead and answer, detective."

She knew LaStanza was prepared for this.

He asked Crystal to repeat the question and answered it with a question of his own, "In Vietnam?"

"No. How many men have you killed in New Orleans?"

LaStanza said, "Unfortunately, I've had to shoot two men in the line of duty."

"Two?" Crystal looked at his notes again. "I've been informed you've shot four people."

LaStanza stared back at Crystal's dark eyes. "Counselor, you've been misinformed."

Crystal shuffled his papers. "Ever been indicted for any of those killings?" He softened his voice when he was most accusatory.

"No, Sir."

Crystal took in a deep breath. "Seventeen police brutality complaints. At least two killings and you're always innocent."

If Crystal was trying to get a rise out of LaStanza he'd succeeded, but the detective was experienced enough to keep it inside. He kept his face placid as he stared back at the learned counselor.

Touché, old man. A good parry, but I'm not going for it.

Crystal flipped through several pages of notes and declared, "I tender the witness."

Judy Brown had two questions in re-direct.

"Were the shootings you were involved in investigated by a Grand Jury *and* the F.B.I.?

God, he wanted to add the words — *meticulously investigated*, but settled for a simple, "Yes, Ma'am."

"And all of the shooting were deemed justified?"

"Yes, Ma'am."

Judy sat back down and the judge dismissed LaStanza, who stepped over to the defense table to re-claim his seat next to Judy Brown. This was the first time he'd ever sat at the prosecution table. A new Louisiana law allowed the chief investigating officer to assist with the prosecution, instead of cooling his heels in the hall where witnesses were sequestered, not allowed to observe the testimony of other witnesses.

He took out his note pad and pen, in anticipation of passing Judy a note if any of the witnesses said something that waved a flag at him. The next witness was the crime lab technician who processed the crime scene.

LaStanza leaned back in his chair and let his mind wander back to the crime scene ...

August 24, 1981
South Rocheblave Street

The rain had ended, but the ground was still soaked as LaStanza stepped away from his unmarked Ford LTD. Moving through the grass alongside the flooded street, amid the constant hum of high speed vehicles flying overhead on the elevated I-10 Pontchartrain Expressway above South Rocheblave, LaStanza stopped when he saw the dumpsters. Dozens of them, some rusty, some in fairly good shape, all lined beneath the overpass.

The only illumination came from the lights from the interstate and the flashlights of the cops standing between the first two dumpsters. A patrol sergeant waved his flashlight at LaStanza, who recognized the big man immediately. Sgt. Ferdinand Thomas was six-three, a former NFL linebacker with skin as dark as burned wood. Stepping over to Thomas, LaStanza spotted three homeless men standing next to a burning oil drum, their faces glowing in the drum's firelight.

"Your victim's about twenty yards that way." Thomas pointed beyond the drum. "Your perpetrator's sitting the back of my unit."

LaStanza turned back to the street and saw a shadow in the back seat of the sergeant's marked NOPD car.

"He say anything?"

"Nope."

"Can you take him up to the Bureau? My sergeant's waiting."

"Sure." Thomas waved a patrolman over as LaStanza walked through the dumpsters, past the burning oil drum, the three homeless men staring at him. Two whites and a black man, all middle-aged, all wearing too many clothes for a summer night. The acrid stench of the fire followed LaStanza.

The victim lay on his right side, white male, forties, full beard, about six feet tall, skinny, wearing a navy pea-jacket, several shirts and very worn blue jeans. He also wore jungle boots, Vietnam-issue combat boots with camouflaged canvas sides.

"Welcome to Fort Dumpster," Sgt. Thomas said as he arrived with his oversized flashlight.

"What?"

"Most of these guys are vets. That's what they call this place."

LaStanza went down on his haunches next to the victim and examined the man's crushed skull with his flashlight.

"What was he hit with?"

"Witnesses say a rock. Perpetrator threw the rock across the railroad tracks after he rifled the victim's pockets."

Standing, LaStanza looked back at the three men next to the oil drum. All wore parts of uniforms, one a marine jacket, one an army field jacket with a familiar patch on the left shoulder, a big red one. First Infantry Division. LaStanza's old unit in Nam.

A crime lab tech arrived and began processing the scene, taking photos, taking measurements, gathering evidence. LaStanza had him search for the rock along the railroad tracks while he spoke with the witnesses.

The men smelled of B.O. and beer, were filthy and hungry and among them had been awarded nine combat citations, including three Bronze Stars for valor. LaStanza learned the accused and victim had each had received a Purple Heart,

11

each had spilled their blood in combat in the defense of their country.

Sgt. Thomas pointed out the dumpster of the accused. It was blue with only a couple rust spots. Tattered railroad ties, stacked outside the dumpster, provided steps to the open top. Leaning inside with his flashlight, LaStanza looked into Michael Bellinger's world, dominated by the sour smell of sweat. Cinder blocks stacked as steps led into the dumpster. A large red and white Igloo ice chest sat next to the cinder blocks. A mattress to the left was piled with several mis-matched blankets. A piece of cardboard above the Igloo had a Silver Star and a Purple Heart medal pinned to it.

Jesus. A Silver Star. Heroism in the face of the enemy.

LaStanza closed his eyes and felt a wave of heat wash across his face, probably from the exhausts from the vehicles overhead and for a moment he was back along the Mekong River, on a patrol trudging through the jungle. Suddenly the birds stopped chirping and everyone hit the deck as Charlie opened up, the bark of AK-47s clashing with the American M-16s. The leaves around LaStanza shredded, the air filled with the chocking stench of gunpowder, along with the coppery scent of blood.

The firefight lasted only ninety seconds. LaStanza emptied three clips from his M-16. They found the bodies of six North Vietnamese regulars in the brush. One G.I. was killed, a kid from Omaha who, that morning, had traded his C-ration chocolate to LaStanza for the free cigarettes that came with the rations.

LaStanza remembered feeling so helpless looking down at the body of the kid from Omaha. Now, as he stood looking down into the accused Michael Bellinger's dumpster, he had the same heart sinking feeling.

Only he wasn't helpless. He took in a deep breath. Helpless, no. He had a job to do. The victim shared a dumpster with another vet. It looked almost the same as Bellinger's without the Silver Star.

When the coroner's office removed the victim's body, LaStanza took his three witnesses to the Detective Bureau for his sergeant to take their statements while he interviewed the accused.

March 5, 1982
Criminal District Court, New Orleans

After the Crime Lab Tech finished explaining how he found the murder weapon, the rock with blood and hair on it, the following morning by the railroad tracks and Harry Crystal passed on cross-examining him, Judy Brown stood up.

"The people call Dr. Matthew Patrick," Judy said as she straightened her black suit coat. She wore a long skirt long, past the knee, a white blouse and low heels, also black.

Patrick was even taller than Crystal and spoke with a New England accent. A retired U.S. Navy officer, Patrick had headed the pathology department at Bethesda Naval Hospital before retiring to New Orleans, where he worked part-time for the coroner. LaStanza felt lucky when one of his victims fell under Patrick's knife because the victim had the best pathologist helping catch his or her killer.

As Dr. Patrick rattled off his credentials, LaStanza glanced at Judy Brown's morning newspaper on the table next to her note pad. There was a picture of John Belushi on the front page. As discreetly as he could, LaStanza opened the paper and let it lay there and felt an immediately stab inside. Belushi found dead. *Found dead?*

LaStanza steeled his reaction from the jury but couldn't stop the sickening feeling in his heart. What a loss. Belushi was so damn funny. He looked for details in the news article and it sounded like an O.D.

Dammit to hell. The man was a comic genius.

He closed the paper and looked at the jury. Three were watching him and he tried his best to keep his face from expressing anything. It was tough. The last time LaStanza felt this way was when John Lennon was killed.

As Dr. Patrick went over the wounds on the victim's body, LaStanza paid close attention. The abrasions were recent and were probably made by a sharp metal object.

Harry Crystal jumped on the knife wounds immediately in his cross-examination, but Dr. Patrick sat there coolly, reciting what he'd said earlier. The abrasions were recent and were probably made by a sharp metal object.

Glancing again at Michael Bellinger, LaStanza saw the defendant wasn't watching Dr. Patrick either. He was staring straight ahead, blinking occasionally. Of all the murderers LaStanza had arrested, Bellinger was the most genuinely sorry for what he'd done. He'd said so right off the bat at the Detective Bureau.

August 24, 1981
Detective Bureau, South Broad Avenue

Sitting behind the small table in a tiny, windowless interview room, on a hard wooden chair whose front legs had been sawed down a half inch so the interviewee was constantly leaning forward, constantly uncomfortable, Michael Bellinger wore his green army field jacket with a yellow and black First Cavalry patch on his shoulder.

The interview was short and to the point. I'm sure ole Jack Webb would describe it as "Just the Facts." LaStanza read him his rights and Michael said, "I killed Pigsticker 'cause he stole from me."

"Pigsticker?"

"Shoemaker's moniker in Nam 'cause he hunted pigs in country. He was a Marine, up by Da Nang when Charlie came outta everywhere. You know. Tet."

The Tet Offensive, 1968.

Bellinger, forty-two years old, was also in Nam during the Tet Offensive. He'd been living at Fort Dumpster for three years. His hazel eyes looked tired, his face hardened by years of sun and wind, his cheeks sunken, his beard scraggly, hair a bushy spider web of brown and gray fibers.

"Pigsticker was always stealing things. Stole food all the time. Stole the ten bucks I got from cars passing on Tulane at Jeff Davis Parkway. I just snapped when my French bread was gone."

Bellinger had spotted a cook tossing out nine loaves of French bread behind a Canal Street restaurant, took them back to the fort and divvied them out, keeping two for himself.

"I caught Pigsticker with a mouthful 'a bread. Said it was part 'a his, but he ate all his. I found summa my ten bucks in his pocket after he was dead. Five dollars and fifty-seven cents. He took my clock too."

"Clock?"

"Little alarm clock I found in a bin behind a motel on

Tulane. Glass chipped, but it still worked. Kind you gotta wind up."

"How did you know he took these things?"

He shrugged.

"Did you see him?"

"I didn't have to." Bellinger looked into LaStanza's eyes. "I knew."

LaStanza saw a look in the man's eyes, a look he'd seen before in the eyes of a sniper he'd photographed outside Bien Hua in a little part of Nam called The Iron Triangle. It was a sudden, sharp look, a snake-eyes look of certainty.

LaStanza stuck to the facts and Michael Bellinger gave them up with no problem, a full inculpatory statement, the kind the D.A.'s Office loved. Bellinger said he was sorry and almost broke down.

"I don't know." Bellinger sat with his head in his hands. "I just snap sometimes. Got this violence in me." He looked up at LaStanza. "Were you in country?"

"Yep. Toward the end."

"Oh."

After LaStanza turned off the tape recorder, he tried to get Bellinger to talk about Vietnam but the man shook his head. He tried to get Bellinger to talk about Fort Dumpster but all Bellinger said was, "When do I get to eat?"

March 5, 1982
Criminal District Court, New Orleans

The first eye-witness took the stand wearing a blue suit the D.A.'s Office bought for him at K-Mart. Louis Bishkin, white male, forty-five, formerly of the First Infantry Division, Bien

Hua, South Vietnam, looked as out of place as the accused in his ill-fitted suit. Red-faced with a bluish drinker's nose, Bishkin was the star witness, the most eloquent when describing the killing.

LaStanza watched him carefully, following his testimony with the statement Bishkin had signed the night of the murder. He'd known of a simmering feud between Bellinger and Shoemaker, cutting remarks about the Marines and Cavalry, accusations of thievery.

As much as he could, LaStanza watched Bellinger, who continued staring straight ahead, seeming to be in another world.

"It was ten-thirty exactly when the fight started," Bishkin said as he began a blow-by-blow description of the fight. LaStanza looked back at Bishkin's original statement and noticed there was no mention of time. In fact, Bishkin originally said he wasn't sure of the time. LaStanza made his first note for Judy Brown.

He followed Bishkin's testimony carefully and there was no further elaboration. He fought off a yawn as Judy sat down. He handed his note to her and she shrugged. OK, witnesses often expanded their testimony once on the witness stand, once they were the center of so much attention.

Harry Crystal's cross-examination of Bishkin was surprisingly short. No need for the jury to dwell on the moment of death.

As Judy started to rise, LaStanza grabbed her arm and pointed to his note. She shrugged again and he leaned over and whispered, "Just ask him." When she leaned back she looked him in the eye and he narrowed his, feeling pin pricks along the back of his neck. It was another of those inexplicable gut feelings a detective gets.

Judy stood and said, "One question on re-direct."

Judge De Salvo nodded.

Judy turned to Bishkin. "How did you know the exact time?"

"Oh." Bishkin smiled and pulled out a small alarm clock from his coat pocket and showed it to Judy. "I looked at my clock."

LaStanza could see the chipped glass on the clock's crystal from where he sat. The pin pricks became needles. LaStanza turned to Bellinger who finally looked at Bishkin, then looked at LaStanza and they both knew it immediately.

He'd killed the wrong man.

THE CASE OF THE STOLEN MEMORIES: A SPADE CONUNDRUM

KRISTINE KATHRYN RUSCH

This original Spade Conundrum short novella is really powerful, as are all the Spade and Spade/Paladin mystery stories and novels. They are great mystery stories set in the science fiction conventions of old.

And Spade might be one of the most original characters in all of mystery.

Kristine Kathryn Rusch is a New York Times and USA Today bestselling writer and maybe the most award-winning and prolific writer working today. She has won more awards in science fiction and mystery than just about anyone alive and she is the only person to win the Hugo Award for her writing as well as her editing.

She writes under three major names, Kristine Kathryn Rusch, Kris Nelscott, and Kristine Grayson. Plus a few minor names.

You can find out a lot more about Kris's work at her publisher, WMG Publishing Inc www.wmgpublishinginc.com or her website www.kriswrites.com

THE CASE OF THE STOLEN MEMORIES: A SPADE CONUNDRUM

KRISTINE KATHRYN RUSCH

He brought them with him, his old friends. Every convention, Ira Hartmann carted his Kodak Carousel slide projector and hundreds of slides into the suite he had sweet-talked the con com into providing for him. Ira was a member of First Fandom, an organization founded in 1959 to bring together science fiction fans of the "golden era"—the pre-1938 era.

Why 1938? Because of the Great Worldcon War of 1939. At least, that was what Ira called it, and I had adopted the terminology, because I'd first learned about the 1939 Worldcon first from him.

My name is Spade. I've been around fandom long enough that most people believe I know everything about everything fannish, but I don't. I am just old enough to have spanned a couple of eras. I knew a lot of members of First Fandom, and I also knew people who should've been in First Fandom, and I knew writers from the Golden Age, and I knew writers from just a few years ago.

Most folks would not say I'm a sensitive soul, but I kinda sorta am. I knew that there were topics the First Fandom folks did not like discussing. Ask Ira about the Exclusion Act at NY Con 1 (as its detractors called that first Worldcon), and he'd give you a sad look. Then he'd change the subject and happily tell you about how he was standing outside the "pavilion" when he spied "this kid from California," who just a few years later would "become" Ray Bradbury.

To hear Ira tell it—all of it—those early years, the 1930s, were glorious. Yeah, they were kids, and no, they didn't have money, but they all loved each other and they all loved science fiction, and Hey. Spade, look at what we built, kid. Look at what we built.

What they built. A network of conventions that had been going around the country ever since that very first Worldcon in 1939, a gathering place for people who loved science fiction, people who loved reading and books and movies and games and all kinds of things that were shunned back in Ira's day.

Ira's day. I was never really certain what Ira's day was. The man was impressive as hell. He was an ambitious talker— probably an annoying one in 1939. He'd been fifteen that year when he met some of the most important people in his life. He became an agent for some of them—I like to imagine this punk kid, talking to big-time editors all of whom I imagine looked like Perry White in the oldest of the old Superman comics— square jawed, loud-talking, salt-and-pepper hair and a take-no-guff persona.

Yeah, kid, yeah. But tell me, kid, why ya think we should waste ink on that story, huh?

Come to discover, years later, that the editors Ira was selling stories to weren't much older than Ira himself. In fact, some of them ran that first Worldcon, and a couple of them might've caused the split heard 'round fandom.

I don't know all the details because I don't want to know all the details. Most of the folks involved were friends of mine —elderly friends of mine who would stiffen up whenever anyone mentioned that first Worldcon.

All those years later, it was still a source of great pain. Hell, during one of the First Fandom Hall of Fame Award presentations at a Hugo ceremony in the 90s, the two factions almost came to blows—and we're not talking young people. We're talking people in their 60s and 70s screeching at each other about something that happened decades ago.

I'd been working security that night. I had to pull two men apart before they broke bones in their hands trying to punch each other. Still, they both ended up with black eyes and one might've lost a tooth or two.

There's a lot of dirt back there, stuff I don't want to know about my heroes. I watched too many of them grow clay feet over the years. Some because of their boorish behavior and some because of stories about them that I simply can't get out of my head.

Modern sf has epic wars, but most of them are online now. I try to avoid them. Back in the day, though, the stuff got hashed out in person. Or in APAzines (amateur press association mimeographed fan magazines). Or in rumor and inuendo.

It was as bad then as it is now. It just didn't happen quite as fast. It didn't go from incident to kerfuffle to picking sides to hatred in the space of a few hours. Usually it took weeks, sometimes months.

Yeah, fandom stuff can get serious. And it lasts. The friendships last, and the enemies last.

Ira knew that. He did his best to avoid the controversies. I can imagine scrawny little Ira, talking his way past all the "older" members of what would become First Fandom, ducking punches and deciding to placate the feelings of others, probably doing it with an overflow of words.

Ira was always overflowing with words—except that morning.

That morning, I saw an Ira hardly anyone saw. Maybe his wife, back when she'd been alive. Maybe a couple of his friends. Maybe.

He had been sitting on the bed in his suite, hands on both sides of his head, body hunched. He wouldn't answer when anyone talked to him, and finally Doris Xavier, who'd been running con security, sent for me, thinking maybe I knew who his family was.

When someone hits their eighties, which Ira was that day, folks suspect severe illness before they think of anything else, which I think of as not all that fair, really, particularly I age.

That morning—that case. I don't talk about it.

Or I didn't.

But Ira's gone now. SF isn't quite the same as it was. Half the eras that I spanned are no longer there. I'm inching into the older generation and I gotta tell you, it's weird.

In those years, Eschercon took place in April. They moved it when a larger convention—with comics and movie stars and some really good cosplay—kept eating away at their membership.

But April—not really the best month to hold a convention in Upstate New York. Either we'd have snow or slush or ice or some damn storm that would delay arrivals. Except the locals who knew which train to take, and who didn't mind getting picked up at the train station by a fan who couldn't drive worth a damn.

I always flew in, because at the time I lived in Seattle proper. I'd made my millions from Microsoft (I'm one of the original Microsoft millionaires), the Victorian I'd bought near the university had quadrupled in value, and I had only just started thinking of selling it.

I'd actually considered going to NY, because so many of my fannish friends lived there. So I was working as many NY conventions as I could, getting to see the back parts of towns that no one normally saw.

The hotel where Eschercon was in those years was the strangest hotel I'd encountered—at least to that point. The local fen (the fannish plural for fans) called it the Escher Hotel, and it was how the con got its name.

The Escher Hotel was really three hotels mashed together. You'd walk down a hallway on the fourth floor and suddenly the carpet would change color and according to the signage you'd be on the eighth floor. Stairways led nowhere, and the third floor rooms in one part of hotel would dead-end into a blank concrete wall which had once been the outside wall of one of the mashed-up hotels.

To make things even weirder, the hotels stood on a definitive corner, where three (former) villages met. That inter-section was the place where street names and zip codes changed. Each hotel was in a different village, and to this day, I have no idea what village the intersecting parts of the hotel(s) stood in.

That year, Ira's suite was on the top floor of the newest hotel, where the guests of honor were staying. I had a suite on that floor too, not because I was special, but because I had money to burn, so I burned it—at least at conventions. I believed in comfort more than anything else. Still do.

So it didn't take me long to get to Ira's room. Doris was hovering at the door, looking nervous, and some sweet young fan, a pretty girl of a type that Ira always seemed to attract, hovered with her.

The sweet young fans, as Doris and I called them, were arm candy for Ira. He was still stubbornly faithful to the wife he'd married at 19, and who had died of some awful cancer twenty years before. But he liked to pretend he was a ladies man, and maybe, by his gentlemanly standards, he was.

"What's going on?" I asked as I barreled through the door.

Forgot to tell you that I'm more Nero Wolfe than Sam Spade. I'm not fond of orchids and I do leave my house and I don't have an assistant named Archie who runs into danger, but I am large and imposing and I like my creature comforts more than I like dishing out a punch.

I don't usually barrel either, but someone had said there was a problem with Ira, and for Ira, I barreled.

Doris stepped to one side and the sweet young fan looked at me like she'd never seen a fat man run before.

"I can't get Ira to tell me what's wrong," Doris said, sounding worried. Doris never sounded worried. That's why I liked working with her.

I glanced at the sweet young fan, about to tell her to go somewhere else, when I realized she was rubbing her hands together. Apparently, that gesture is called wringing, although for the life of me, I've never understood it.

"I came to get him for brunch," she said. "The door was open."

Her voice got a little louder, a little more insistent.

Someone had probably already questioned whether or not she had spent the night in the room.

Ira never fought the perceptions of his manliness, unless it got the sweet young fen in trouble. Then he was Sir Galahad, ready to ride in on a metaphorical horse.

"I called his name, and he didn't say anything." She bit her lower lip. "I went in farther, and there he was."

She waved a hand at the bedroom, and my heart clenched. At that moment, I hadn't seen Ira yet, didn't know that he was hunched, didn't know that he was even alive, although I figured Doris would've told me if he wasn't.

I pushed past the sweet young fan and barreled toward the bedroom. I know CPR. I've had to use it, but I was afraid to use it on Ira. He was still a small man, and in his eighties, he had become frail.

I wasn't sure I'd be able to do the compressions without shattering a bone.

But I didn't need to. Ira sat on the edge of his bed, his head bowed, his shoulders shaking, clearly alive.

I let out a gusty sigh of relief and walked over to him. I put my meaty hand on his shaking shoulder and said, "Ira, it's Spade."

He didn't acknowledge me.

That was when I realized he was crying. And, as I looked around the room, I noted that the bed was made, and the old-fashioned he'd brought with him for a nightcap the night before was still sitting, untouched, on the nightstand. The ice had melted long ago, the bitters had settled on the bottom, and the whiskey wasn't that golden any more, given the amount of water now in the glass.

Ira used drinks like that to help him sleep—or so he said—

and I'd watched him down plenty before turning in. Ira was from that generation: he was a drinker, and proud of it.

I crouched. My knees cracked so hard I thought they probably heard the snap in New Jersey. I peered up at him. His hair, usually manicured away from his face with some sickly sweet gel, had fallen across his cheeks. His hands looked glued to his skin.

"Ira," I said again. "Ira, look at me."

He didn't. He wouldn't. I wasn't even sure he saw me.

I turned, straining my back. I would never get out of this position again, I was sure of it.

"Doris," I said none too loudly, because she was hovering near the door, the sweet young fan behind her, "call 911."

"No." The word was barely audible. A croak, really.

I looked back at Ira. He still hadn't pulled his hands away from his face, but he was sitting up a bit straighter.

"I'm okay," he said, even though it was clearly a lie.

He finally let his hands drop. His large nose was red, his eyes were puffy, and his cheeks were chapped.

His lower lip trembled, and that's when I realized he'd been crying. Crying for hours. The kind of crying that people did when someone died.

"Spade, you stay." Then Ira attempted a smile, maybe even one of his charming smiles, and said to the sweet young fan, "Honey, I'm skipping brunch, okay?"

"You sure?" she asked. "I mean, food would probably help—"

His smile had a bit of an edge now. I saw the Ira who had become a big Manhattan lawyer, who had given up fandom to negotiate deals in TV and theater when New York City was the center of the entertainment universe.

He had only come back to us after he retired and his wife died. And then he never mentioned all the things he had done in the name of entertainment. Just what he had been doing in sf before he had Become Somebody.

"Honey," he said in a way that made it clear that right now, he couldn't remember her name, "don't you worry about me."

She didn't notice. She was still hovering. It didn't matter how pretty or seemingly normal fen were, they were still fen. And there were reasons she was in the sf crowd. Apparently her inability to read a room was one of them.

I turned even farther so I could give her hand signals that I hoped she could understand. He's okay and Go away. I didn't quite make a shooing motion, but I almost did.

Doris took pity on her. Or on me. Doris took the sweet young fan by the arm and helped her out of the room as if she was the one in trouble, not Ira.

Then Doris pulled the door closed, and I collapsed onto the floor. My knees were not meant to hold all 400 pounds of me in a crouch for that long.

Ira frowned at me.

"You okay?" he asked with a bit of an edge. On the one hand, it was typical Ira. He was concerned for someone else, always, wanting the best for people, always, but on the other hand, it was Ira the Lawyer. You okay, because I gotta situation here.

"Just needed to plant my butt on the floor," I said as if I did that every day.

It actually got a small smile from him.

"Tell me what's going on," I said, and the small smile faded as if it had never been.

His lower lip started trembling again. "My slide show. It's gone."

My turn to frown. "Did you leave it somewhere?"

"Yeah," he said. "Here. In this room. I already did the show, Spade. You didn't come."

"I'm sorry," I said automatically. That tone—slightly blaming, slightly accusing—reached into a part of me that had once been smaller and less sure of himself. My mother used to use a tone like that when she had been disappointed in me, and that's what it felt like now, with Ira.

He waved a hand as if my lack of attendance didn't matter, even though it clearly did.

I wasn't going to tell him the truth, not about that. I only caught every third show that Ira did at conventions, because mostly, they were the same—Ira walking down memory lane, telling stories that were fascinating the first three or four times. The show was best when we were in a place like New York, which had First Fandom members heavy on the ground, and they could fight or argue or challenge Ira's memories. Or add to them.

I learned a lot about the early days of sf from those verbal tussles. He was right: I should have been at this one. I had forgotten all about it.

"It wasn't good," he said. "It got heated."

He always thought the contentious "shows" were the worst ones, primarily because they made him uncomfortable.

I had met the Hartmann clan on more than one occasion and when they got together, Ira's word was law. They all loved him—from the middle-aged adult kids down to the littlest of grandchildren—but no one disagreed with him.

I was pretty sure that the only place that anyone disagreed

with Ira was in the tight little hotel rooms at various conventions, when his Kodak Carousel took center stage.

"And you're positive that you brought the entire show back to the room," I said, because I had to clarify.

"Spade, do I look like a schlemiel to you?" he snapped.

Since my only encounter at that moment in my life with the word schlemiel had been in the opening credits to Laverne and Shirley, and I never knew what it referred to, I figured this was not the time to guess. So I did not respond to the question exactly.

"Ira," I said. "I would ask the same thing of anyone. Sometimes we get distracted, especially if your panel was heated."

"It wasn't a panel," he said sullenly. "It was a presentation, and I got interrupted. A lot."

He hated getting interrupted. He took the interruptions personally sometimes, as if people were discounting his memories. Longtime friends knew how to ask questions or volunteer their memories in a way that wouldn't anger him and derail the presentation.

"Who interrupted you?" I asked.

He waved a hand. "It's not important. What's important is that I got here, I put my equipment on that table over there—"

He continued to wave his hand, this time indicating the round table that most hotel rooms had as a "dining" table. This suite had an actual dining table in the very large living/dining/kitchen area, so this table was just an extra.

"—and then I went to dinner." He peered at me. "You remember dinner, right?"

It was a passive aggressive jab, the kind I'd heard Ira use with his kids and some of his longtime friends, but never with me.

"It was a lovely dinner," I said. "Of course I remember it."

And if I didn't, my black American Express card would have reminded me at the end of the month in the form of a charge of $750 for the five of us who had been there.

"The soup could've been better," Ira muttered.

"It could have been," I said, mostly to get him back onto what actually happened.

"I had a drink with..." And he waved his hand again, this time to refer to the sweet young fan, whose name I couldn't remember either. "...and then I came back up here. Alone."

He eyed me as if to reinforce the point. I knew he never brought the sweet young fen back for after-hours romping. I'd actually checked on Ira's activities with younger women. There weren't any. When I ran security at various conventions —something I hadn't done in a long time now—I made sure that whatever looked suspicious wasn't suspicious or criminal or had happened with consent.

With Ira, there was no need for consent, because he always walked the ladies to their doors—and left them there, in the hallway, before he toddled off to his own suite.

"You walked her home first, right?" I asked.

"Not last night," he said. "She retired early. I was talking to Ava Walters."

When Ira "talked" with Ava Walters, it was never really talking. It was shouting and fist-pounding and disagreements that could never be settled.

I'd seen photos of Ava back in the day, and she looked like Ava Gardner's not-quite-photo-ready sister. Same curvy figure, same big eyes. But Ava Walter's hair was always clumped or falling out of its pins, and she never did manage the art of make-up.

She had grown into a round woman who looked like some-one's really nice mother (or grandmother these days) until you looked at her eyes. A glance from those eyes was enough to bring anyone to their knees.

She and Ira fought like cats and dogs all the time. But, from the things Ira said sideways when she wasn't in attendance, I got the sense that she was the one who got away.

"Did you settle anything?" I asked.

He glared at me. The look wasn't as powerful as usual, given his red tear-stained eyes.

"I had some new slides," he said. "She claims I mislabeled them."

"New slides?" I asked, unable to keep the surprise out of my voice. He hadn't had new slides in all the years I'd gone to the presentation. He had different slides, ones that would go in and out of the rotation, but never anything new.

"If you had come, you would've seen," he said.

"I'm sorry I missed it," I said, finally able to apologize with sincerity. Because I was sorry I missed the new slides. "What were they?"

"My son was cleaning out our basement," Ira said, "and he found an entire box I'd put there and forgotten about. I have lots of new slides."

I processed all of that information. Cleaning out the base-ment of old items in the house an 85-year-old man had shared with his long-dead wife sounded more like cleaning out the house itself.

"And before you ask," he said, "yes, I'm moving. My son found me a place in his building."

His son lived in one of the newer condo complexes in Midtown. Very upscale and posh. I knew that Ira could afford it, but I was surprised. He had said he never wanted to leave the memories.

A shiver ran down my back. Maybe there was more to the tears than the lost Kodak Carousel.

"He insisted that I have a housekeeper come in every day." Ira's lips formed a thin line. "I guess he didn't like how the house was looking."

I gave him a sympathetic smile. "He wouldn't like how my house looks either, Ira."

Ira smiled at me, but it was perfunctory.

"So he's moving things, and found the slides," I said.

"And I've been labeling them," Ira said. "I'm going to donate everything when I go."

I knew that. He was having trouble finding a place for his memories, though. He'd thought of going to the newly established Science Fiction Hall of Fame, but it was too pro-focused for him. Even though the Hall of Fame was founded by a subset of fandom, they really didn't seem to respect the fannish community. And there were other problems as well.

I'd backed the project initially, but was seeing the nightmarish handwriting on a very political wall. So I stepped back. Ira had asked me a few times to help him find a university to take his things. I'd suggested the Eastern New Mexico University in Portales, but Ira made a face every time.

Which baffled me, because that collection was anchored by Portales resident Jack Williamson, who was also First Fandom-eligible (whether or not he'd joined, I had no idea) and who was a decorated, important science fiction writer, who'd been published in every decade since the 1920s.

I never asked, although it seemed impossible to me that anyone would dislike Jack. I guessed, though, it was Portales or New Mexico. So far from the coasts and what Ira believed to be the Real World that I had a hunch he saw it all as also-ran.

"I brought out some of the new ones for the first time yesterday," Ira said. "I passed the word. You didn't get the word?"

I hadn't, but that didn't mean much. My attendance at cons was always more about running them in those days (heck, and in these days too) than it was about attending panels.

"I've been spending most of my time in Con-Ops this convention," I said.

"You," Ira said, wagging a finger at me, "need a life."

I nodded, because I didn't want to disagree with him. I considered convention going and sf fandom my life. But Ira still believed in the 1950s American Dream. He thought I needed a wife to take care of my household and at least 2.5 kids.

I once made the mistake of telling him no woman would have me, and he spent the next con-year trying to fix me up with his sweet young fen.

"The slides," I said, trying to focus him on the problem. Trying to control a conversation with Ira was like trying to wrestle an aging but canny tiger.

He slid to the edge of the bed, so he could lean closer to me. His eyes actually lit up.

"They are of the 1939 Worldcon," he said. "They're valuable. My father gave me a Canon Rangefinder, and spent a small fortune, let me tell you."

Ira's father was one of the few who made money during the Depression. Ira would never tell me what his father did, but I looked it up. His father had a hand in the illegal alcohol industry and, like Joseph Kennedy, had entire boatloads (literal boatloads) of European booze ready to sell the night Prohibition ended.

"I spent another fortune in film," Ira was saying, "and developed it all after the convention."

He grinned. The grin relieved me more than I could say.

"People called me obnoxious because I was always sticking a camera in their face. That whole weekend. They kept calling me a pesky kid. One of them threatened to take the camera and smash it over my head."

I raised an eyebrow, Spocklike. "Do you remember who that was?"

"I wanna say it was Fred Pohl, because Fred had a lot of secrets, you know?" Ira said. "I'm not sure he was faithful to Leslie, even then. And he was a communist. You knew that, right?"

Fred Pohl was another of sf most famous early writers. Fred's personal history was colorful to say the least. He had been married five times, and there were a lot of rumors about other women, particularly in the 1940s (when three of his marriages occurred). He had been a member of the communist party in the 1930s, when he was a teenager and renounced the party about the time of the first Worldcon. He went on to serve in an elite Air unit in World War II, something I never heard him talk about.

Nor did he say much about his controversial years as a literary agent, although a lot of people hated him because of it. And his years as an editor.

Fred never showed up at any of Ira's talks, and I often wondered about their relationship. They never sat near each other, even when they were both in the green room at a con before a panel, and I didn't recall them ever exchanging words about anything.

It would make sense if their relationship was contentious. I sometimes saw the questionnaires that went to author guests, where they could ask to avoid other writers or fans, and Fred's had some really well known names on them.

Ira never filled out one of the questionnaires because he only did his slideshow. He refused to sit on fannish panels, but that was something that only the Secret Masters of Fandom who ran conventions knew. Ira tried not to say anything bad about anyone at a convention, which made his comments about Fred—sideways as they were—unusual.

"You say you wanted to say it was Fred, but you're not saying it was Fred," I said. "Was it Fred?"

Ira shook his head. "I thought it was, the day it happened. But turns out it, it was Mervin DeGrastene."

That was a name I had never heard before.

"Who?" I asked.

"Nowadays you'd call him a Big Name Fan," Ira said. "He was at every East Coast gathering before the war. And he looked a lot like Fred. Everyone said so. It really made Fred mad, too, because Fred got blamed for some of the things that Mervin did. When I think about it now, I wonder if Mervin encouraged the confusion."

I felt a little off-kilter. I had thought I knew everyone who had been part of science fiction in those early years. Or at least knew of them.

"What happened to him?" I asked.

"Mervin?" Ira frowned. "I don't know. I just stopped seeing him around."

"When?" I asked. "Before the war?"

"We all served, Spade. There was no during the war, and after…" Ira shook his head. "A lot of us became grown-ups after. Put away our childish things."

He gave me a sad smile. I knew part of this history, but I let him say it.

"Unfortunately, many of us saw sf as a childish thing," he said.

"Did you?" I'd never really asked him that before. I'd heard a number of reasons why he left fandom. Most people said it was because of his wife. She didn't approve at all.

He looked down at his hands. I looked at them too, twisted and swollen with arthritis. He saw my gaze and put them on his knees as if he was trying to stretch the fingers out.

"You don't know what it was like after," he said. "We built a peaceful world for you kids."

I waited. I'd heard that before. The world wasn't peaceful. I grew up in the Cold War, and it was scary. Small skirmishes and border wars always felt like they could spill into something much bigger and much more sinister.

But I was also aware that our generation had been spared the world-wide terror that had been the Second World War.

He shook his head, as if he was testing sentences and rejecting them.

Finally, he said, "Look, Spade. After the war, we, none of us, were the same. We'd seen things…"

I waited. His gaze still wasn't meeting mine.

"…and then there was the bomb. We did that. Science did that. Science wasn't this joyful benign thing anymore. I mean, even Jack Williamson came out of that war wondering how any of us could glorify science anymore."

I never thought of the early writers as glorifying science,

although that was an element of sf from the beginning. Ira was right, though; 1950s' sf was decidedly darker than any we'd seen before, but that was true of every literary aspect of the 1950s. And movies too.

"So," Ira said, "a lot of us, we went on to other things."

So there it was, why Ira really left sf. It was easier to say that his wife forced him to do so. Pieces of Ira and parts of the stories he told fell into place now.

"The new slides," I said, changing the subject back. "They're all of the 1939 Worldcon?"

"No," he said. "But the ones I brought here are. They're from the local meetings and from the Worldcon and from just some of the get-togethers."

"And Ava was at those?" I asked.

He shook his head. "Not all of them."

"She angered you, though."

He gave me a sad smile. "She always angers me. I worry about you as a detective, Spade, if you haven't noticed that."

"Enough to be bothered by the interruptions at your presentation," I said.

"She approached me after the presentation," he said.

"So who interrupted you there?" I asked.

"Well, Sam," he said. "But Sam always interrupts me. He has to remain the authority on the history of sf, you know."

Again, with the bitterness. Which didn't surprise me with Ira's relationship to Sam Moskowitz. Sam was considered the authority on the early history of science fiction. He was the guy who barred several Futurians from entering the 1939 Worldcon. Sam. The authority.

The Futurians were a group of sf fans, many of whom ended up being truly influential in sf. People like Fred Pohl and Don Wolheim (who founded DAW books). Sam was a member of the Futurians until real-world politics got in the way. Most of the Futurians at that point were members of the Communist Party, which Sam did not like...or something like that.

As I said, I'm never did learn all the details. I liked all of these people, even the most contentious ones, and I'm educated enough to know that folks who flirted with Communism in the 1930s didn't really understand what the party was.

Especially teenage folks, which almost all of them were.

I never asked Ira which side of the great divide he fell on, but he probably wouldn't have told me anyway. But given the way he and Sam fought, I often wondered if Ira identified with the Futurians in that argument.

Although, in the 1950s, when Ira became a high-falutin' lawyer, being affiliated with the Communist Party in anyway was dangerous. And Ira had fingers in Hollywood, which meant he could have been called before the House UnAmerican Activities Committee if he so much as sneezed wrong.

I understood the caution then. Not so much now. Although I knew that the habits of a lifetime often became ingrained.

"Who else interrupted you?" I asked Ira.

He shrugged and looked down. I had never seen that kind of response from him before. He usually deflected a topic he didn't want to discuss by changing the subject.

"If you want me to find the carousel," I said, "then you need to tell me everything."

He raised his head, his eyes still lined with tears. "There is no everything, Spade. Some of us just disagree, is all. We've disagreed for sixty years. The fen were fighting when I left sf to go to war, and they were still fighting when I came back ten years ago."

"But it bothers you," I said.

"Yeah," he said quietly. "But not so much as Ava."

My legs were cramping up. I needed to get off this floor, but we had finally gotten to the meat of this discussion. I didn't dare move yet.

I waited. I wasn't sure if he was responding to "bother" in the literal sense or in the sense that she bothered a part of him that he didn't like to acknowledge after his wife's death.

"She says..." His voice trailed off and he looked down again.

When it became clear he wasn't going to say anymore, I spoke for him. "She said that you didn't label everything properly on the new slides. Do you believe her?"

"NO!" He startled himself when he shouted, and actually scooted back a bit on the bed. "Sorry, Spade. Sorry."

It was clear from that kind of outburst that we were actually getting somewhere.

"What did she think you mislabeled?" I asked.

"If we had the slides, I could show you," he said.

"Do you still have the photos themselves?" I asked.

"Yes," he said. "Where'd you think I got the slides?"

"Are the photos here?" I asked.

His bushy eyebrows came together in a frown. "I had the slides. Why would I need the photos?"

I was groping at something. "Do other people know that you still have the photos?"

"I didn't say it, exactly," he said. "Not that it would've mattered to anyone. Sam thought the pictures were unimportant."

"But Ava didn't," I said.

"Oh, she didn't talk about importance," Ira said. "She pointed out—repeatedly, I might add—that I once again confused Fred with Mervin."

I tilted my head a little. "You'd done it before?"

"No," Ira said. "She always thought I did, though."

"Why is that important to her?" I asked, mused, really. Then I saw the stricken look on Ira's face.

"Why? I thought you were a detective, Spade. All the little details in everything, they're the most important." Ira leaned back just a little. He had forgotten about the theft, at least for the moment, and that made him calmer.

"Fred doesn't come to your presentations," I said. "What about Mervin?"

Ira barked out a laugh. It wasn't a laugh at my expense or anything else. Instead, it was a laugh of surprise.

"I thought you knew fannish history, Spade," he said.

"I do," I said.

"Then you know that Mervin DeGrastene never made it to the war. He died in Queens about a month after that world-con." Ira lowered his voice. "Everyone thinks he was murdered."

There was a lot to unpack in those three sentences. I started with the most obvious one.

"Was he murdered?" I asked.

"He was nineteen, and he died because he hit his head. The police thought he tripped and kiboshed himself on a table."

"But you don't," I said.

"None of fandom did," Ira said. "But most of us didn't know nothing. I didn't even hear he was dead for two weeks after."

I nodded. I felt a little chilled. I had no idea that anyone had been murdered in fandom. I didn't think of us as a particularly violent bunch. Even the Great Worldcon War never really came to blows. Ira and Sam agreed on that at least.

Murder. It happened in our community like every other community, although not at cons. Like Barbara, who ran a comic book store in Michigan. She was murdered just a few years before this conversation, and later (much later) her husband was convicted, and it all became fodder for a Dateline episode a few years back, because of the sf/comic connection.

The mention of an old homicide, though, got me thinking like the detective I'm supposed to be.

I asked, "When you introduced the new slides, did you mention that they were part of a group of slides you just found or did you not mention that at all?"

"I didn't say I found them," Ira said stiffly. "I said my son happened upon them. An entire box. A big box."

I shifted slightly, wishing I could stand without being rude.

"And you said there'd be more in future presentations?" I asked.

"Yes, Spade. That's just good marketing. You know that."

"Are the photos protected now?" I asked.

"Protected?" Ira's voice went up. "Protected? What do you mean, Spade?"

I didn't mean to upset him further, that was for certain. But I was. Still, I needed answers to these questions.

"Where are they?" I asked with trepidation. "At your house?"

"No," he said, and shook his head for emphasis. "I gave

them to my son. He's having them all converted to slides at my request."

"This is David, right?" I asked. Ira had three sons and a daughter. I had just been assuming that the son who had the pictures was the son who lived in Manhattan.

"Yes, David. Everyone else left New York." Ira said that as if he couldn't believe anyone would make that choice ever.

I let out a small breath.

"Why?" Ira asked.

"Noodling," I said. "The other slides, they have photographic backup too, right?"

Ira's lower lip started trembling again. "No. I thought you knew that. My wife made me keep them in a storage unit and it got flooded in the 1970s. Negatives, everything. Gone."

By the end of that speech, his voice was trembling too. That was what disturbed him about the loss of the slides.

He couldn't replace them.

He leaned forward and grabbed my hands, startling me.

"They're all I have of those years," he said. "All I have of those friends. It's how I…"

He shook his head, and that movement shook a tear loose.

"I understand," I said, and I thought I did. I do understand more now, as I'm writing this, even though I'm still not even close to 85. But Ira is gone now, as are so many others of my friends, and all I have of them are memories that no one else shares.

I couldn't—and can't—imagine the weight that a gregarious 85-year-old felt when faced with continual losses spread over decades.

"I'll find them," I promised. Stupidly. Real life detectives, police officers, and others—they never make promises like that.

But I did.

Ira squeezed my hands again.

"It's okay, Spade," he said. "My son, David, he tells me I gotta let the memories go. I can't keep everything that reminds me of something."

He choked on the last few words. Then he swallowed and continued.

"I'm trying, Spade. I really am." He gave me a watery smile. "Getting old. It ain't no picnic."

"I know," I said. I was sincere, even though, in hindsight, I didn't know at all.

———————

Okay, I'm ashamed of this next part, but I'm going to tell it anyway.

After I managed to get Ira to head downstairs to join the sweet young fan for a belated brunch, I went to Con Ops. That was where my Tower of Terror lived.

I brought some of my computers with me everywhere. They were large towers that held disks and data and had hard drives and all kinds of what were then more powerful than any locomotive that other desktops had. I always have state-of-the-art computer systems because of my Microsoft days, and back then, I ran everything in Con Ops from those Towers of Terror.

On a Sunday morning, Con Ops had an eerie resemblance to the Marie Celeste—the ghost ship that was discovered that looked like everyone had vanished midmeal. There were candy wrappers everywhere, open cans of Coke, Dr. Pepper, and every other soft drink you could think of except the zero-calorie kind, as well as coffee cups scattered across every surface, except the one holding my computer.

The folks who ran conventions learned long ago that the only time I ever showed anything like wrath was if someone brought food or drink near the Towers of Terror. In that, I was the 1970s Lou Ferringo Hulk, only without the body builder's muscles. Just the Bill Bixby catch phrase:

Don't make me angry. You wouldn't like me when I'm angry.

I was one of the first people ever to move my paper Rolodex onto my computer. And because I had a lot of confidential information from my days as a forensic accountant, I had the thing password protected at the NSA level.

But I also kept every phone number and piece of contact information I ever gathered, and that included the contact information for Ira's son David, acquired when we were planning a non-con dinner in Manhattan a dozen years before.

After I found the number, I wrote it on a piece of paper and took it up to my room. I didn't want anyone to overhear the conversation and have it get back to Ira. Even though Con Ops was empty that Sunday morning, I knew it probably wouldn't remain empty for long.

My suite was smaller than Ira's and not as tidy. After five days of almost no sleep (I generally arrive at cons I'm working at on Tuesday), I can't be expected to clean up past picking my underwear and dirty t-shirts off the floor.

Housekeeping hadn't arrived yet, so I sat on one of the flimsy chairs in front of the so-called desk that this room had and punched David's number into the hotel phone.

To my surprise, David answered on the second ring.

"Pops?" he asked.

"Um…no," I said. "It's Spade."

After I got the name out, I wasn't sure if he would remember who that even was.

"Oh, Dad's detective friend. It's been a long time." David's voice was wary. "I expected a call from Dad from this number."

Apparently, David had put the hotel's number into his Caller ID.

"He okay?" David asked, and that was when I twigged to the worry. David was afraid that something would happen to his father, alone at an sf convention.

"He's a little emotional," I said, "but otherwise all right."

David let out a sigh of relief. "So this is about…?"

I told him about the missing carousel. I also asked him not to tell his father that I had called.

"I'm looking into what happened," I said. "But before I conduct an actual investigation, I need to know something."

"What?" David sounded wary all over again.

"Your father," I said. "How's his memory?"

"My father?" David asked, sounding incredulous. "You're asking about my father?"

"Yes," I said. "He mentioned his moving out of his house and I was wondering if it was because, you know, of health issues?"

"You're asking if he has dementia." David laughed. "Seriously. My father. No, Mr. Spade. He doesn't have dementia. He's the guy who remembers every time I farted at the dinner table from 1972 through the present."

I chuckled because I was supposed to.

"His memory is fine. The move is his idea. The house is too big for him, and I think something spooked him. He tripped or he dropped something or maybe he just realized that a house like that is a landmine for the unwary." The laughter had left David's voice. "He's moving into my building, but still will have his own place. With fewer traps for the unwary. The tough part is getting rid of all the family heirlooms. I made my siblings promise to take their fair share, even if they put the crap into storage. Otherwise Dad wouldn't have moved."

I understood that. I had no idea what would happen to my possessions after I no longer had use for them, but I wasn't willing to part with them—not yet, anyway.

"Thanks," I said. "I was concerned. Your father calls these memories, and I wasn't sure if his memories were stolen by a person or by time itself."

"Naw," David said. "My father's memory is as sharp as ever, maybe sharper. I wouldn't argue with him about anything, Mr. Spade. He has more room in that brain than anyone I've ever met."

I nodded, feeling embarrassed. I hadn't trusted my own instincts with Ira. I always thought he was a man who forgot nothing, but I let his age and one small detail about his life shake that perception.

But I did need to know whether or not he had gotten absent-minded. Or worse.

And now I did.

"Listen," David said before I could end the conversation, "don't tell my dad but someone broke into the house this morning. That's why I don't want him to live there."

Now, he had my attention. "Did they take anything?"

"Naw," David said. "My dad has the nosiest neighbors this side of a Bewitched episode. Their version of Gladys Kravitz called the cops and they arrived within five minutes. Dad's not going to have that kind of service in Manhattan, let me tell you."

"Was someone arrested?" I asked.

"Stupid small borough cops," David said. "Arrived with sirens blaring and lights flashing. No, of course they didn't catch anyone. Not sure they wanted to."

I thanked him, frowning. Old detectives in books always said there were no coincidences, but you live long enough and you realize that there are a lot of coincidences.

Just not here. I was pretty sure that break-in and the loss of the carousel were tied together. I needed to find that carousel before whoever took it had a chance to destroy it and all the memories contained in those little 2" x 2" slides.

————

To start, I needed Doris's help. I hadn't worked much with the Escher Hotel on that year's Eschercon, so I had no contacts there. I needed to know something that I wasn't sure they could tell me.

I found her in the Green Room, settling an early morning fight between two Big Name panelists. Each wanted to moderate the 10 a.m. panel and use it to force an agenda that the other disagreed with.

I didn't have time to wait for the eons' old fight to find some kind of momentary truce. Instead, I beckoned her, told her I thought that Ira's slides had been stolen, and asked her to go with me to the front desk.

She looked shocked and asked the 64,000-dollar question: Who would want to steal those slides?

I told her I didn't know, even though that was half a lie. I had a small idea as to who might have stolen them, although that plus the break-in at Ira's house did take the theft to a level I hadn't expected.

Doris grabbed Carole B, who was making sure that the Green Room snacks were being replaced (particularly the coffee) and assigned her the task of getting the Big Names to their panel.

Then Doris led me to the front desk, and asked for the manager. When she arrived, all official in her suit jacket, except for a tiny Superman pin that she must have gotten from Julius Schwartz, one of the most influential editors from the Silver Age of comics, who handed the pins out to anyone he liked or who had done him a favor. The pin endeared her to me. She could have just thanked him and put it in her desk.

"We had a theft in one of the rooms," Doris said quietly, even though no one was near the front desk at the moment.

Most of the fen had Monday checkout, so they could stick around for the Dead Dog Party. Those who didn't had late checkout, and hadn't even gotten up yet.

The manager looked disturbed and was about to ask a question, when Doris continued, "It was a targeted theft. Only one very precious item was taken."

I could see dollar signs flashing over the manager's head. How much liability did the hotel have? What would this do to their reputation? What if the culprit was someone on staff?

So I stepped in. "The item had value only to the person in the room. And obviously to the person who stole it. We're not talking about the Hope diamond or anything."

To her credit, the manager's expression didn't change, although her shoulders visibly relaxed.

"What do you need from me?" she asked.

Doris looked at me. I'd thought for a while how to phrase this question.

I gave the manager Ira's room number and said, "I need to know who had a key to that room."

The manager immediately jumped on the computer and dug up the information. "It looks like the couple staying there have the only two keys."

She was referring to actual keys, not key cards. Back then, only the high-end hotels in the biggest of cities had them.

"Couple?" Doris said. "Do you have the right room?"

The manager repeated the number to her. "That's the room, right?"

I put a hand on Doris's arm, stopping her. "When did the wife pick up her key?"

The manager clacked a few keys. "Yesterday at five-thirty."

Not long after Ira's presentation finished. And a half an hour after the group of us met for dinner. We'd been loud and laughing as we headed over to the most expensive restaurant in the Escher complex.

A lot of people would have noticed us.

"Did she leave her name, by chance?" I asked, knowing it was a long shot.

She thinned her lips. "Your questions are making me wonder what's awry here."

"Ira's a widower," Doris said.

"And he's not prone to taking other women into his room or to giving out his key," I said.

"Someone's going to get in trouble for this," the manager said.

"Don't," I said. "It's not your desk's fault."

"They should have checked identification," the manager said.

"And probably did," I said. "Many people in our community don't share last names. I'll wager the woman who got the key was of an age with Ira, so your employee thought nothing of the request."

"You're being charitable," the manager said. "I think we should call the police."

"Not yet," I said. "What's been stolen has no physical value. So the police won't really pay attention."

The manager frowned at me.

"I would like to talk with the person on the desk last night, if I could," I said.

"He won't be in until 2," the manager said.

I hoped to have everything wrapped up by then, but I didn't mention that. "Do you have a security system? Maybe a camera pointing at the desk?"

"We don't record," the manager said. "Privacy concerns."

I resisted the urge to look at Doris. I'd been telling her that the Escher Hotel was getting rough around the edges, but that comment confirmed it. Hotels usually didn't care about that kind of privacy unless they knew their hotel was being used for illegal hook-ups or other shady businesses.

We thanked the manager and left the desk. If my assumption was correct, my suspect pool was small.

"What do you want to do?" Doris asked me.

"I'm going to talk to a few people," I said, "and then I'll let you know."

The first person on my list was standing, bleary-eyed, at the coffee and pastry spread that this convention was famous for. So many fen didn't want much more than that for breakfast. They wanted to grab something quick and head to their panel.

I excused myself and walked over to the table. I grabbed a paper plate and covered it with a cherry Danish.

"Ava," I said to the woman next to me. "Can I have a minute?"

She blinked at me. "Oh, the pretend detective man," she said.

I made myself smile. "That's me."

"For the record," she said. "I didn't do it. I claim credit for all of my crimes and I haven't committed one since I got here."

"Good to know," I said. "But I don't want to talk to you about crimes."

"Oh?" she asked.

I could see Doris out of the corner of my eye. She looked surprised too.

"Let's just grab a seat," I said, waving a hand at one of the seating groups at the far side of the lobby.

"You got fifteen minutes, Big Boy," Ava said, and picked up a coffee to go with her plate full of croissants. I took a water. I'd get something caffeinated later.

We walked across the lobby to the pleather chairs. No one was sitting there, although a few more fen were emerging from the nearby elevators, looking as bleary as Ava had.

"I wanted to talk to you about Ira's presentation," I said.

"You don't get to yell at me, kid," she said. "Ira's been passing off his memories as the truth for years now."

"I'm not going to yell," I said. "I want to know about the new slides. You said he got a few things wrong."

I didn't add that it bothered Ira, because she already knew that. Besides, I wanted the focus to be on the slides, not on Ira.

"Oh," she said, "he's been doing it for years."

"What's that?" I asked.

"Confusing Fred Pohl with Mervin DeGrastene." She took a bite from a croissant and immediately pastry flakes covered her gray I'm old, not stupid sweatshirt.

"Why does that bother you?" I asked.

She frowned at me, then leaned back. Those eyes were sharp. "Does this have anything to do with Ira's sad face this morning?"

"Very good deflection," I said, hoping I could deflect as well. "Please, just answer the question."

She looked down, saw the pastry flakes, and wiped them off the front of her sweatshirt. I got the sense that she didn't want me to see her reaction.

"Look, kid," she said, "details matter. It matters that he confuses them."

"Why?" I asked. I almost said, They're his memories, after all, but that would make this about Ira. I had a sense it was something more.

She sighed. "You're not gonna let this go, are you?"

"No," I said.

She looked up, and all pretense was gone from her face. I saw a tired woman who, in her own way, looked as sad as Ira did.

"No one remembers Mervin, not really, and I'm not sure they should."

"Then why did you bring it up?" I asked.

"Because his pictures need to be excised from all writings about fandom," she said with such viciousness that I almost leaned back.

"Why?" I asked.

"Oh, just ask any other woman who was around then," she said and started to stand.

I reached out and almost grabbed her arm, then decided that was a bad idea. "Please," I said. "I'll work with Ira, if you just tell me what's going on."

"You know Mervin was killed, right?" Ava said as she sank back into the chair.

"I just found out this morning. I heard it was an accident."

"Accident schmaccident," Ava said. "In my day, someone'd call that justifiable homicide."

I stiffened. "What happened?"

"I honestly don't know for sure," Ava said. "But I do know cops investigated and talked to half of the women in fandom at the time. Which was probably three of us."

She let out a bitter laugh.

I waited, because what else could I do?

"He did the same with all of us," she said. "We don't talk about it. I didn't go near men for a long time after that, not that anyone noticed or cared. And then the war, and there were other things…"

Her voice trailed off. But her eyes remained defiant.

"You know, Ira always thought I pushed him away because of him. In those days, Mr. Pretend Detective, women didn't talk to anyone but other women about men like Mervin. We warned each other to stay away."

She still wasn't saying exactly what happened, although I could guess.

57

"He hurt you," I said, deciding to be as elliptical as I could.

"Oh, hell, no," she said. "Hurt is not the word you young people use. He took what he wanted and I couldn't fight hard enough. Clear enough for you?"

My cheeks were flushed. I wasn't going to use the word rape if she wasn't. I didn't want to shut her down.

"Clear," I said.

"And there was one of us," Ava said. "I know she went to Mervin's apartment that day, voluntarily, because I couldn't talk her out of it. I also know she was a mess for years, and I know that she once asked my husband—a career prosecutor in the City—if you shoved someone and they died, was that a homicide?"

"What was his response?" I asked.

She glared at me. "I loved my husband, but he wasn't the most sensitive man in the history of the universe. He said, depends on the circumstances, but unless you called the police and reported it right away, it would probably be considered manslaughter at best."

I let out a small breath. Manslaughter. "Do I know this person?" I asked.

"Yeah," she said. "And it isn't me, if you were wondering. But that's all you'll get out of me."

I nodded as if that was okay, which, on some level, it was.

"The photos, what did they show?" I asked.

"Have Ira show you," she said.

"I can't," I said. "Someone stole the carousel."

I didn't tell her that the same someone had a friend or friends break into his house to find other pictures.

"Oh, for Pete's sake," she said, then let out a sigh. "The photos weren't of Fred and his latest patootie, which is what

Ira said. I pulled him aside later, said he was disrespecting Leslie—"

Leslie Perri, Fred's first wife, whom he met in fandom around that time, and who had died long before I entered fandom.

"—and he needed to cut it out. Fred always had women, but he was faithful when he was married." Ava sighed. "Ira's just jealous. Fred could attract women by doing nothing. Ira had to work at it. And before you ask, I was not one of Fred's 'patooties.' God, I hate that word. But Fred and me, we still don't get along much."

"Yet you're defending him," I said.

"I'm not," she said. "He just shouldn't be confused with that piece of filth Mervin."

"So who was the woman he was with?" I asked.

"C'mon, Mr. Pretend Detective," she said. "Two plus two shouldn't be that hard for someone like you, especially since she got scared and actually stole the evidence."

"Evidence of what?" I asked.

"Unless I miss my guess," Ava said, "that photo was the last one taken of Mervin alive."

In all my years investigating small crimes at sf conventions, I'd never had a fictional detective moment before—y'know, where the pieces fell into place so quickly that a chill ran down my back. I'd also never dealt with an actual death before, even if it happened years before I was born.

Ava was right. Two plus two wasn't hard. And she was

wrong about one thing. There were more than six women in those early years of sf, although not all were members of First Fandom or even came back to fandom after the war.

But Evelyn Chastain had. In Ira's photos, she looked like a tiny bird with great taste in clothes, always wearing a dress with a flare skirt and low heels that made her look like a 1930s movie star, until the camera caught her face and couldn't get past the thick glasses to reveal her eyes.

Evelyn still wore thick glasses, but on a birdlike elderly woman they looked appropriate.

I found her in the hallway outside a panel on the roots of modern science fiction.

"May we talk?" I asked.

She hobbled toward me, her walker barely keeping her upright. At least it was the proper height. She was maybe five feet tall these days and so thin it looked like she could disappear if she turned sideways.

"You haven't destroyed Ira's carousel yet, have you?" I asked.

She looked at me sharply, and nearly lost her balance. "How'd you know?"

I could've told her about the things I'd discovered, but I didn't. I also knew she had the means and the wherewithal to hire someone to break into Ira's house and take that box.

"I talked to the front desk," I said. "They believed that Ira's wife asked for an extra key. The young man at the desk would've believed that only a few people here were married to Ira."

She let out a sad laugh. "Age wins again," she said.

"Did you destroy it?" I asked.

"No," she said. "Not that it matters."

"It matters to Ira," I said. "His memories are in there."

She leaned one arm on the walker and tapped her forehead with the other. "His memories are in there."

I shook my head. "Ira's a little different than most people. He likes to see his memories in black-and-white."

Her mouth thinned, but she didn't say anything.

"If I get Ira to promise not to show any pictures of Mervin DeGrastene," I said, "will you return the carousel?"

"Ira confuses Mervin and Fred," she said quietly.

"I know," I said. "You have no problems with the old slides. Just the new ones, right?"

She raised her tiny chin. "You know why," she said with a touch of incredulity.

"I know nothing," I said. "Except that as far as the police are concerned, Mervin's death was labeled an accident, and there's no open case file."

"And that matters how?" she asked.

I wasn't a lawyer. I'm still not. But I do think about justice sometimes.

"As I see it," I said, "there's four potential crimes here. One attempted but thwarted, one that would've been charged the way a prosecutor told you years ago and a modern jury would've considered self-defense. Then there's a minor theft of valueless Kodak carousel, and a more serious break-in at an elderly man's abode."

Her eyes narrowed. The movement seemed larger than it was, thanks to her thick lenses.

"It seems to me," I said, "that the only one today's police would care about is the break-in. Then they'd want to know why, and they'd start digging in places that don't need any investigation at all."

"Is that a threat?" she asked, her voice wobbling just a little.

I hunched, trying to make myself less threatening.

"No." I made my voice as gentle as possible. "I suspect whatever happened—"

"It was self defense!" she said so loudly that all five people in the corridor (two Klingons, a hotel employee, and two not-yet-famous writers) looked at us.

"I know," I said, and let the words hang.

She stepped closer to her walker, as if she felt wobbly, but I knew better than to touch her.

"I'm not going to say anything," I said. "And other people, who've suspected for years, haven't said anything either."

"Then how do you know?" she asked.

"I pulled it out of the wife of that prosecutor who scared the crap out of you," I said.

Evelyn smiled at me. "You think you can get me to confess."

"To the carousel, yes," I said. "The rest of it, there's nothing to confess."

She looked down at her walker, then said, "You know, Ira and I don't agree about much. He thinks the history is so danged good. He thinks we were all so happy. None of us were happy. That's why we banded together. We needed something else to talk about besides having no money and what was going on in Europe."

I waited.

Then she looked up at me and shrugged. "I should never have gone to his presentation."

I nodded.

She squared her thin shoulders. "If I give him back the

carousel, can you make sure he doesn't use the slides of Mervin. That bastard doesn't deserve to be mentioned as part of fandom."

"I think I can do that," I said.

"Without telling Ira what happened," she said.

That would be harder, but I had a hunch I could do it.

"Yes," I said.

"I don't want to talk to Ira," she said.

"You don't have to," I said. "You still have his key, right?"

"Yes," she said.

"Let's just put the carousel back in his room."

Which was what we did. I had to tell Ira that I dealt with the culprit, so that he wouldn't worry that he had somehow missed seeing the carousel. I didn't want him to suddenly be concerned about his own mental health.

Then I lied to him. I told him that Fred still didn't like being confused with Mervin and it would be better for all if any Fred or Mervin pictures weren't in the presentation.

"I can do that," Ira said so quickly that I realized that the history between him and Fred was as touchy as I thought it might have been.

At future cons, Ira used new slides, but kept his promise. And he also kept his carousel locked up in the hotel safe at night.

He never asked me who took the carousel. He was just happy to get it back. I'm not sure if Ava told him. I know Evelyn didn't. Until the end of her days, she remained true to her word. She never showed up at one of his presentations again.

They changed, those presentations, particularly after more and more of the original members of First Fandom passed. Ira removed the slides that used to anger Sam after Sam died. Ira added a few gorgeous slides of Ava after her death—loving shots that I think he never ever showed her.

A few weeks ago, Ira died. His son David called me and offered me the entire slide show.

"I thought your dad was giving it to the Science Fiction Museum," I said.

"They want someone to go through it," David said. "I don't have the heart or the knowledge."

So Ira's slides—Ira's memories—are spread out over my kitchen table. I'm going to digitize them to preserve all of them.

But I keep staring at one of a birdlike woman who was no one's patootie next to a man who bore a slight resemblance to the young Fred Pohl. Only that man had ice-cold eyes, and hands the size of meat hammers.

I like to think I would have seen Mervin DeGrastene for what he was if I ever met him, but I'm not sure any of us ever see others for who they are.

The histories that Ira knew and conveniently forgot, the undercurrents among a group of young adults who had no idea what kind of hell their generation was about to face, are lost now. Some of the faces in these shots I don't recognize, and the people who could've identified them are gone too.

There are candid shots that aren't going to the museum and some photographs that'll never see the light of day because of my conversations with Evelyn and Ava.

Ira left me his memories so that I could sort them, and make sure they didn't hurt anyone. Ira had cleansed them, made them harmless, made his friends harmless, and took all the complexities out of their young lives. The good, the bad, and some of the ugly.

Stories. That's what he trafficked in. That's what he turned his memories into. Stories that comforted him and pretended that everything was right for a brief shining moment in the world before it spiraled into a nightmare.

Because for him, that's what the moment was. Even with the Great Worldcon War, that he ignored. The Exclusion Act, the split in his beloved fandom, the fact that most of these kids continued their fight long after it ceased to matter.

It was small. It was easy to focus on. It allowed them to ignore the pain of life mid-century.

I get that now, and I want to talk to him about it.

But of course, I can't.

A QUIET NEIGHBORHOOD

ANNIE REED

Professional writer Annie Reed writes stories that span genres and are always powerful. In fact with Annie, you just never know the type of story you might be reading, but you will always know it will grab you and be a compelling read.

With this story, Annie sets an amazing scene of 1950s America. A lost culture, brought forward by this great crime story. So far Annie has had a story in every issue of Pulphouse Fiction Magazine and as the editor, I hope to continue that streak.

Annie's stories have appeared in four best mystery stories of the year volumes so far. Look for so much more of Annie's work at her website https://anniereed.wordpress.com/

A QUIET NEIGHBORHOOD

ANNIE REED

The house had been built in the '50s, back in the days when Detective Kyle Beecham's parents were bright-eyed teenage newlyweds who still believed in the post-war American Dream. Two kids, a dog, and a new car in the drive-way, and dinner on the table by six—pot roast, gravy, and mashed potatoes, canned green beans and a slice or two of white bread. A tiny television in the living room, ashtrays on the dining room table. Everyone smoked, no one cared about things like lung cancer or heart disease or high cholesterol, and things looked rosy—so long as you were white and male and gainfully employed.

Reno had still been small in those days, and Sparks, Beecham's hometown, had been little more than Reno's bedroom community. Neighbors left their doors unlocked, and kids played unmolested in the streets. Most houses came equipped with single-car garages, and front yards came standard with one tree and stubborn lawns that never did quite take to Northern Nevada's summertime heat.

Beecham hadn't grown up in that era, but he'd heard often enough from certain fellow officers nearing retirement how glorious life had been back then compared to now. He'd been a late-in-life child born in the '70s to parents who'd long since given up on having kids of their own. His mother used to call him a surprise when she was feeling kindly; a mistake, she'd said, when she wasn't, which was most of the time.

He'd lived his whole life in Sparks, and Sparks was his beat. He knew the neighborhoods, especially the old neighborhoods like the one he'd been called to on this snowy January evening.

The standard front-yard elm tree had been dug up long ago, not even a stump left behind. The lawn had been replaced with decomposed granite and evergreen shrubs, all covered now with a light dusting of snow. Decorative plaster yard animals—a doe curled up around her fawn; a seagull perched on a pier piling; a racoon sitting on its haunches—nestled in next to the bushes. The animals hadn't fared well over the years. The doe's haunches were caved in, and the snow flurries were settling in the cracked remains of the raccoon's tail. The shrubs were overgrown, with dried weeds poking through the branches.

Clumps of leaves from neighboring trees had settled around the bases of the shrubs and the edges of the sidewalk and driveway. More sodden leaves clogged the gutter and stuck to the bottom of Beecham's shoes as he walked from where he'd parked his department-issued car across the street to where a crime scene tech was working in the front yard.

According to the weather app on Beecham's phone, the sun had set only a few minutes ago, not that he could tell thanks to the heavy cloud cover. The streets were still mostly slush.

When the temperature dropped in another couple of hours, the slush would turn to ice. Patrol officers were going to be busy tonight responding to accidents.

The house he'd been called to had an air of aged neglect. The light next to the front door only gave off a weak, yellowish glow that did little to illuminate the raised cement slab that served as the house's front porch. A few of the siding shingles on the front wall were cracked and chipped, and the trim around the windows was warped. An old-fashioned wall-mounted mailbox next to the front door was stuffed with grocery ads and junk mail.

The place might have looked nice at one time, back when whoever lived here had the energy and money to keep the place up. Beecham could almost see what it had looked like in its day.

Yellow crime scene tape had been strung across part of the front yard. The tape marked the edge of a line of blood drops leading from the front porch to the split-rail fence that separated the front yard from the sidewalk. The crime scene tech had strung up plastic sheeting over the blood trail to keep the blood from dissolving any further in the wet snow, but she was fighting a losing battle.

A breeze kicked up from the west, rattling the crime scene tape and the sheeting, and blowing the falling snow sideways. The tech muttered a few choice curses as she shifted her body to try to block the wind from sending falling snow beneath the sheeting.

Beecham turned up the collar of his overcoat. He really should wear a hat on nights like this, but he'd never gotten in the habit. He bent at the waist, hands braced on his knees, to get a closer look at the blood. Indentations next to a few of the drops looked like footprints, but in the decomposed granite, the indentations weren't as clear as he might have liked.

"Get a photo of those?" Beecham asked the tech.

The woman nodded without looking up from her work. "Gonna be a bitch trying to get a match," she said. "Not that you'll need it."

Beecham raised an eyebrow. He'd worked with this tech before, and she rarely voiced an opinion about one of his crime scenes.

"Anything you want to share?" he asked.

She gave him a long look from beneath the hood of her down jacket. She was a small woman, maybe a hundred ten pounds, if that, and the puffy coat looked at least three sizes too big. Combined with her short, dark hair, dark eyes, and somewhat pointed chin, the hood gave her face a pixie-like appearance, like someone from one of the animated shows Beecham's daughter liked to watch on television.

The tech started to say something, then stopped herself. "You'll see," was all she finally told him.

Beecham grunted and straightened up. "Good call," he said. He preferred his own impressions of a crime scene, not impressions filtered through someone else's opinions. She knew that, but she was probably just grumpy because of the weather.

Besides himself, two patrol officers had responded to the scene. The lights on their black SUVs lit up the street. The body transport van hadn't arrived yet. The EMT truck was already gone, no doubt called away to deal with someone who was still living.

One of the patrol officers stood on the porch next to the

front door. The cheap hollow-core door was closed, but it had been splintered near the lock.

"You do that?" Beecham asked the officer.

The man was one of the newly minted officers hired during the department's last bump in personnel, thanks to the town's ever-increasing population, a side-effect of the cluster of mega-factories east of town. From what Beecham had heard, this particular officer had served two tours in Afghanistan before he'd applied to the academy. He was a solid six feet tall, all muscle, no fat.

"Yes, sir," the officer said. "No response to my knock. I saw the body on the floor through the window and what looked like blood."

The patrol officers had responded to a 9-1-1 call of a woman screaming, possible domestic disturbance. In a situation like that, kicking in the door was a reasonable response.

Beecham knew the layout of these houses like he knew the back of his hand. The door opened directly into the living room. The over-sized front room window that looked out over the porch wasn't exactly floor to ceiling, but close. A couple of weeks ago that window would have been the perfect spot to display a Christmas tree. Tonight, the opening in the drapes on that window gave him a perfect view of the body on the living room floor.

"Any civilians inside besides the deceased?" he asked.

"Just one," the patrol officer said. "Elderly female. She's—"

Beecham held up a hand to stop the officer from saying anything else. He hadn't worked with the man before, so there was no way the officer could know Beecham didn't want to know anything about possible witnesses except the basics.

"What about the back door?" he asked. "Any evidence of a break in?"

"No, sir. The back door's locked, no sign of forced entry. The garage's been converted to a storage room, wood paneling on all the walls, no outside access except a narrow window at the back. Windows all have locks engaged, no panes broken."

Beecham pressed his lips together in a tight line. No obvious evidence of a robbery or home invasion, although he'd check it all again himself.

"Either of you canvas the neighbors?" he asked, referring to the other patrol officer who'd be inside the house. Patrol officers worked on their own, no partners. Two patrol vehicles meant two officers had responded to the 9-1-1 call. "Any lookie-loos?"

"Not really," the patrol officer said. "Just the guy across the street, keeps looking out his window."

Curious but non-involved. A lot of these old neighborhoods had a mixture of long-time residents and lower-income families looking for starter homes. Gone were the days when all the neighbors knew each other.

"Why don't you go find out what the guy across the street has to say," Beecham said. "Check around with the other neighbors, see if anyone noticed anything."

The patrol officer nodded and took off across the street. Beecham saw the drapes move in the nosy neighbor's house. If the weather had been better, the guy might have come out on the street to get a closer look.

Beecham took a second to stand on the porch before he went inside. The house didn't have the suburban ghetto feel of a drug den or a gang hangout—no empty beer or wine bottles in the recycle bin, no slats missing from the six-foot wooden privacy fence that separated the front yard from the back. No abandoned vehicles parked in the yard. None of the houses in the neighborhood had that feel.

The only car in the driveway was an older model with newish mud-and-snow tires. No satellite TV dish, no big-screen television visible in the living room. The place wasn't an obvious target for a burglary gone wrong—nothing valuable to steal. The street was off the beaten path. Not a single car had driven past during the whole time Beecham had been here. If it had been a home invasion, which the blood trail out front pointed to, the residents must have opened the door to let the invader inside.

Beecham took the small flashlight he always carried out of his coat pocket and turned it on. The overhang from the roof protected the porch from the snow, and the concrete was nearly dry. He saw no blood drops on the porch, no bloody footprints. Any other footprint evidence would have been obliterated by the first responders. He turned the flashlight off and put it back in his pocket.

Nothing else to see out here. Except for the blood trail in the front yard and the body inside, this was just another house in a quiet suburban neighborhood. Not much different from the aging neighborhood only half a mile away where his father had killed his mother when Beecham was nine years old.

———

B eecham was an only child born to parents who, at thirty-nine, had endured more than twenty long years of well-meaning friends and nosy relatives asking, "so when are you two going to have a baby of your own?"

75

His mother had come to take all that pushy concern about the barren state of her womb as a personal failing. In her era women got married and stayed home to raise the children. It was *expected*, after all, and if a woman wasn't actually expecting a child of her own by the time she hit thirty—especially if said woman was married at eighteen—well… it certainly couldn't be the man's fault, now could it?

When Beecham was born in the spring of 1973, a bouncing, healthy, normal baby boy, all those friends and relatives had shot sidelong glances at his mother, like she'd somehow shirked her wifely duties all those years. He supposed, given her general prickly disposition, it was only natural that she transferred all those years of built-up resentment to him.

She hadn't abused him—not exactly. Emotional abuse wasn't really a thing anyone talked about in those days, especially not in a small town like Sparks, and especially not when it came to children. She hadn't laid a hand on him. Instead, she'd been a woman of comments—constant little criticisms thrown at him like tiny emotional knives. Her knives were the sharpest when she'd been drinking, and by the time he was old enough to realize what alcohol was all about, she was drinking a lot.

Beecham's mom threw a lot of her emotional daggers at his dad as well, and he sometimes threw them back. Beecham grew up thinking that's just how families treated each other— long periods of angry silence or short bursts of all-out verbal warfare. He discovered he was wrong when he stumbled across pictures of younger versions of his parents in old photo albums on the bottom shelf of a bookcase in their bedroom. They almost looked like totally different people.

They'd actually been happy people in those photographs,

like the old black-and-whites of his dad holding a trophy with his bowling team or flipping burgers on a backyard grill. Color photos of his parents on the beach at Tahoe, his mom sitting in a lawn chair reading, a bottle of beer half buried in the sand next to her chair, while his dad played volleyball near the water with their friends. They smiled a lot in those photos, and sometimes the photographer had caught them in mid-laugh. They'd even had dogs. Beecham had wanted a dog of his own, but his parents always said no.

His parents said no to a lot of things when Beecham was a kid. His dad never cooked on the old brick barbeque in the backyard, and he didn't go bowling with any of his buddies. They never went on family outings to Lake Tahoe. They played cards with their friends, or his mom would knit while his dad watched television, and always, always, they'd have beer or cocktails while they smoked their cigarettes.

Beecham didn't have any real friends until second grade when he became buddies with a Hispanic kid named Bobby Lopez. Bobby had three sisters, all older, and one younger brother, and they all became Beecham's second family. He picked up Spanish thanks to the Lopez family and learned how to make authentic Mexican food, not the fast-food stuff his mom sometimes bought for dinner when she didn't feel like cooking. If his parents noticed that he was rarely home anymore, they never said anything, and he began to realize that his parents, especially his mom, would just as soon not have him around.

He figured out why one afternoon when he was in the third grade. He came straight home from school instead of going to Bobby's because Bobby had gone home sick. A strange car was parked in the driveway, and when Beecham let himself in with the key he wore on a cord around his neck, a strange man was inside with his mom.

Although Beecham could tell his mom was angry with him, she smiled like she was actually happy to see him. When she introduced him to the man—a friend of hers, she'd said— her voice didn't have the hard edge he was used to.

After that, his mom started going out during the day instead of staying home so she'd be there whenever he came home from school and didn't go straight to Bobby's.

"You're a big boy now," she'd told him. "You should be old enough to be home by yourself after school. I have things to do."

Beecham hadn't minded. He actually enjoyed being home by himself. He started spending as many afternoons after school at home as he did at Bobby's house. Sometimes Bobby came over, but all they did was watch television or play ball or skateboard out front. He didn't care what his mom did with her days, and at first he didn't think his dad did either because they fought less at night. His mom didn't criticize him as much as she used to. Sometimes she even used her happy voice when she talked to him or his dad, and she didn't drink as much anymore.

He'd thought his parents were finally starting to be more like Bobby's parents—happy people who teased each other and danced to the radio and even kissed sometimes when the kids were around. He started to hope that maybe they'd take him to Tahoe one day to play on the beach. He'd learned how to play volleyball in school, so maybe his dad might want to play volleyball with him. Or if his dad didn't want to play volleyball, maybe he'd want to fish. Bobby's uncle fished in the river somewhere east of town and said he'd take Beecham and Bobby along one day, but Beecham's mom always said no.

Then he came home one afternoon a week after his ninth birthday to find the strange car in the driveway again, his dad's car parked across the street, and half a dozen cop cars blocking the street.

———

The living room in the old house was as small as Beecham expected. All the houses in these old neighborhoods had been part of the same housing development back in the '50s, little single-story homes that squeezed three bedrooms, two bathrooms, a living room, dining room, and kitchen into little more than a thousand square feet.

His daughter's bedroom in the house Beecham owned was bigger than this living room. Still, the occupants had managed to squeeze in a sofa, coffee table, two recliners, and an entertainment center, complete with an older model television (not flatscreen) into the living space. The walls were decorated with the kind of mass-produced artwork that had been popular decades ago along with collage-style frames filled with family photographs and a few framed pieces of needlework. A hand-made afghan was draped across the back of the sofa, and a free-standing floor lamp stood in the space between one end of the sofa and one of the recliners. A side table centered in the front window held a large table lamp. The ceiling had been texturized at one time, with little sparkles embedded in the decorative swirls. The shades on both lamps were dusty, with cobwebs trailing down from the ceiling.

The lamps were both turned on, which gave just enough

light for Beecham to get a decent look at the body of an elderly man face down between the coffee table and the television. Blood had soaked into the carpet, turning the olive-green textured pile an ugly brown.

Nothing in the living room looked out of place except the body. Nothing broken, nothing knocked over. No signs of a struggle.

The other patrol officer, a woman in her thirties, stood in the opening between the living room and the dining room, keeping watch over an elderly woman who sat at the dining room table, her back to the wall separating the house from the garage. The woman's hands were encased in clear plastic bags.

"Where did you find her?" Beecham asked the patrol officer.

"On the sofa." The officer nodded at the end of the sofa closest to the dining room.

"You bag her hands?"

"Yes, sir. She wanted to wash them."

Beecham didn't have to ask if the officer had noticed blood on the woman's hands. The plastic bags spoke volumes.

So did the knife on the carpet next to the body.

Beecham crouched down as close as he could to the body without disturbing it. The crime scene tech hadn't been in here yet, thanks to the snow. Better to work the evidence that would degrade with the weather. This body wasn't going anywhere soon.

The victim looked to be in his seventies, at least. His face was turned to the side, the one eye Beecham could see was faded with age. His skin was sallow and heavily wrinkled, and his mostly bald head was dotted with liver spots. The knuckles on his hands were swollen with arthritis. He was slender, probably five-eight, if that, and dressed in casual slacks and a cardigan over a polo shirt, and dark brown penny loafers.

The cardigan had at least five large, bloody stab wounds in the back, possibly more, most in the mid-back area, but one large wound near the top of the man's right shoulder blade.

Beecham turned his flashlight on the knife. Straight-edged, long blade kitchen knife. Blood covered the blade as well as the wooden handle. Smears in the dried blood on the handle showed where someone had gripped the knife. With any luck, the tech would be able to pull a few good prints off the handle.

"Anybody move the knife?" he asked the patrol officer.

"No, sir," she said. "That's where we found it."

And that's where it would stay until the crime scene tech was done with it.

The victim had a plain gold band on his ring finger. Beecham wondered how long he'd been married.

"You get a name?" he asked the patrol officer.

"Records says the property's owned by Harold and Grace Moore, purchased in 1964. The woman responds to Grace—Mrs. Moore." She nodded at a pile of envelopes on the coffee table. "Mail's addressed to the Moores as well, but I don't have a solid I.D. on the victim yet." She cleared her throat. "Didn't want to disturb the body to look in his pockets."

Beecham caught the odd way the officer had referred to the woman, that she "responded to" Grace. "She didn't volunteer her name?" he asked.

The officer's eyes flicked toward the woman, then she looked at Beecham. "She doesn't volunteer anything. I'm not sure she's all—"

The officer stopped herself before Beecham had to say

anything. He'd worked with her before, back when he'd been assigned to burglary. He didn't have to tell her how he liked to work.

He slipped on a pair of latex gloves and leaned forward to pat the man's pockets. No wallet. "Check the bedroom," Beecham said. "See what you can find."

The patrol officer nodded at him and disappeared toward the back of the house through the kitchen.

Beecham straightened up, his knees popping. The older he got, the less his joints liked the cold. Not that it was cold in this house. The thermostat must have been turned up to at least seventy-five.

He took off his overcoat and was draping it carefully over the recliner next to the front window right about the time the door opened and the crime scene tech stepped inside. She'd ditched her bulky down jacket on the front porch before she came inside. Now she was dressed in the sweatshirt and slick pants she normally wore to crime scenes.

"Finished out there?" Beecham asked.

"Damn snow," she muttered. "Got as much as I could, but it'll be enough for a match."

To the victim. She was assuming it was the victim's blood, but there was no trail on the carpet from the victim to the front door or on the porch to the front yard, and the knife—the presumable murder weapon—was still on the floor next to the body. Where had the blood in the yard come from?

The tech pulled on paper booties over her boots and then put on a fresh pair of gloves. She dropped her crime scene kit by the front door and turned her attention to the body. Beecham left her to her work.

There wasn't enough room to walk by the body to get to

the dining room, so Beecham squeezed in between the coffee table and the sofa. A half-empty mug of coffee sat on the coffee table near where the patrol officer had indicated she found the elderly woman sitting. The stench of death had overwhelmed the coffee smell until he was practically on top of the mug. The mug itself looked like handmade stoneware, the type Beecham had seen at the craft shows his ex used to drag him to. What looked like dried blood marred the handle.

"Be sure to bag that too," he said to the tech, pointing at the mug.

She shot him a long-suffering look. "Not my first rodeo, sport."

The patrol officer came back into the kitchen holding a man's wallet in her gloved hand. Beecham took the wallet from her and looked inside.

The vic's name was Harold Moore, age seventy-nine, and he still had a valid Nevada driver's license. No eyeglass restrictions, which at his age probably meant he'd had cataract surgery on his eyes. Not unusual for long-time residents. The Reno area was a mile above sea level. People who didn't take care of their eyes and protect their skin ended up with cataracts and skin diseases in their later years.

"See anything that might identify our witness?" he asked the patrol officer. "Purse? Wallet?"

"No purse that I could see," she said. "The vic's wallet was on top of the dresser in the master bedroom."

"Check it out," he said.

The officer gave him a look that clearly said, "why didn't you ask me the first time?" but she didn't say anything, just disappeared into the back of the house again.

Beecham had an ulterior motive for sending the officer to

do another search. He didn't want a uniformed cop standing in the background while he questioned the victim's wife. There was a reason detectives wore street clothes. Most days Beecham wore suits, which made him look like just another businessman. On snowy days like today, he wore jeans and sweaters beneath his overcoat. The outfit made him look like just another guy in the neighborhood, someone you could tell your troubles to, not an authority figure who might put you behind bars.

He set Harold's wallet down on the kitchen counter. The kitchen was fairly clean, dishes draining next to the sink, a clean, well-used skillet on the stovetop, no dishwasher, an older fridge with a freezer on top. The kitchen and dining room floors were covered with indoor/outdoor carpeting that had gone out of style three decades ago, but the carpet was clean. No food left out on the counter, just a half pot of coffee left warming in a drip-style coffeemaker. A plug-in room freshener in an outlet next to the stove explained the floral scent in the kitchen, an odor that clashed horribly with smell of blood.

He pulled out a chair from the dining room table and sat down across from the elderly woman. She didn't seem to notice him. She sat almost as still as a statue, her bagged hands resting on the table, staring off into the middle distance. She was exceedingly thin, even for an elderly woman. Her fuzzy white hair looked like dandelion fluff that might blow away in a strong breeze. Her brown eyes were faded and deep set in her hollow-cheeked face. Her eyes were red-rimmed, but those hollow cheeks were dry. She had blood smeared on the front of her housedress, but it was hard to see given the dress's dark, abstract print.

"Mrs. Moore?" Beecham said. "Grace?"

She didn't respond to her married name, only her first name. She turned her head toward him. "Do you think I can have a glass of water?" she asked.

The patrol officer had started to imply that the victim's wife wasn't all there, but her voice was calm and measured. She could have been in shock earlier.

"I'll get you one in a minute," Beecham said. "First I need to ask you a few questions. Would that be okay?"

She nodded. Her head shook a little from side to side afterwards, a tremor, not a "no." He wondered if she even noticed.

This close to her he could clearly see the blood that covered both her hands. Like her husband, her knuckles were swollen with arthritis, but her fingers weren't pulled out of shape. Her hands were delicate though, the fingers small-boned just like the rest of her that he could see.

"Did you do the needlework in your living room?" he asked as a way to start a conversation.

Her gaze flickered to the living room but just as quickly flickered away. "Yes," she said, "although I can't do much anymore." She looked down at her encased hands. "Hard to hold the needles, you know?"

The blood on her hands didn't seem to bother her as much as looking at the living room.

"How long have you been married, Grace?" he asked.

She frowned, closing her eyes, trying to remember. "We married very young," she said. "I know that. Fifty-eight years? Fifty-nine? It's hard to remember."

"That's a very long time to spend with someone," he said.

"He's the love of my life." She sighed, and then she smiled.

"The years go by so quickly when you're in love. But you're far too young to know that."

Beecham hadn't expected the smile. It wasn't the self-satisfied smile of a killer or the guileless smile of a person who wasn't quite all there mentally. This was the smile of a woman in love, and it brought a rosy blush to her hollow cheeks and light to her faded brown eyes.

"Do you want to tell me what happened here?" he asked gently.

She turned the smile on him. Now the smile lit up her entire face. "You already know," she said, "or you wouldn't have had that nice young woman do this." She held up her bagged hands. "I killed him. I took a knife from my kitchen drawer and I stabbed him while he was going to check the mail. I didn't plan to, and I made it as quick as I could, but I'm not as strong as I used to be."

Beecham hadn't expected the confession. He'd expected confusion, or a claim that a stranger had killed her husband, that the blood on her hands was from when, in her grief, she tried to revive him.

They'd been married for nearly six decades, and one day she'd just snapped and killed him.

Beecham leaned back in the chair, his blood chilled to the bone. No matter how long he did this job, he would never get used to the idea that people who claimed to love each other could do something like this. Like what his parents had done to each other, although he wasn't sure what they had felt for each other could have been called love.

"Do you think I could have that glass of water now?" Mrs. Moore asked.

Beecham had decided to become a cop because of what happened with his parents. Because of the cops who'd responded to his house after his dad killed his mom and her "friend." Because of the way they'd treated him and tried to protect him.

Beecham had learned, much later, that his dad had been fired from his job that day, the company he worked for a victim of hard times. Instead of drinking away his shock at a casino downtown, he'd come home, hoping against hope to find a little solace in the arms of his wife. After all, she'd seemed happier lately, less caustic. She'd even stopped drinking.

Instead when he came home, he found her in bed with her "friend."

They'd been so involved with each other they hadn't heard him come in, but he heard them. He saw them, and he just snapped.

Crime of passion, the cops called it. Temporary insanity, his dad's defense attorney claimed. Beecham's dad had gone to the kitchen, found the sharpest knife in the cutlery drawer, took it to the bedroom, and stabbed his wife and her lover a combined total of forty-seven times.

Beecham didn't find out all the details of the crime until he'd read the file after he was on the force. He'd been too young, and the killings were over by the time he got home from Bobby's house.

"At least you were spared that," his aunt had said, trying to comfort him, not that it helped.

It took years before he finally quit believing, deep down,

that his mother would still be alive if only he'd come straight home after school instead of stopping by Bobby's house. If he'd gone straight home, his mom wouldn't have still been in bed with her lover. If only he'd gone straight home, her "friend" would have left, and Beecham's dad wouldn't have found the two of them together and gone temporarily insane.

If only he'd gone straight home from school, his dad wouldn't have committed suicide in prison.

His aunt had picked Beecham up from the police station, and he spent the rest of his childhood living with her. She was his mother's younger sister and the mirror image of his mom. A fun-loving closeted lesbian who took in a shell-shocked nine-year-old boy when she'd never planned to have children of her own, she decided to give him the kind of childhood his parents hadn't. She took him on trips to Tahoe, not to mention San Francisco and Seattle and Los Angeles. She treated him like a mini adult, talking to him about politics and music and art, which was her passion as well as her livelihood, and slowly he began to heal.

She died of lung cancer right after he graduated from the police academy.

"Ironic, don't you think?" she'd said when she initially told him the diagnosis. She'd never smoked, not even marijuana, while her sister had smoked like a chimney.

After the cancer had metastasized and chemo no longer worked, she had decided she wanted to spend her last days at home surrounded by her art and her music. Beecham had been by her side when she passed, her favorite Crosby, Stills & Nash CD playing in the background.

He'd cleaned out her medicine cabinet after she died, and he'd been shocked at the number of little pill bottles for treatment of her symptoms. When he opened one of the cabinets in the Moores' kitchen and saw the array of pill bottles and the types of medicine, he began to understand what must have really happened.

By then Mrs. Moore had been transported to the station in the back of a third patrol car he'd called to the scene. He'd read her her rights and cuffed her, keeping to protocol, but she wouldn't try to go anywhere. Why should she? If the medications he saw in the Moores' kitchen cabinet were any indication, she was dying.

They both were.

There'd be an autopsy, of course, and Beecham would subpoena the victim's medical records, but he knew. The victim had cancer, what kind didn't really matter, and the prognosis hadn't been good.

Cancer was a slow, agonizing death. He'd witnessed that with his aunt, and she'd been the most full-of-life person he'd ever known. She hadn't begged him to end it, no matter how bad the pain got. Her art and music kept her going.

Had Mr. Moore begged his wife to end his suffering? Had she begged him? Beecham didn't think so. There were easier ways to go, like an overdose of the pain pills that had been prescribed for each of them. They'd simply stoically endured their fate, been the quiet, elderly couple the nosy neighbor across the street described, until she'd snapped.

She'd killed him to end his suffering. She said she hadn't planned it, and he'd clarify that point when he interviewed her at the station to get an official statement. She simply couldn't take watching the man she'd loved for six decades suffer one minute longer. If she'd been stronger, it would have taken only one or two attempts, but in the end she'd killed him in a frenzy, stabbing him in the back because as much as she loved him, she couldn't have killed him if she'd been looking in his face.

As for the blood drops in the front yard, Beecham had a theory about that. The police had found his dad in their back-yard next to the old brick barbeque. He was still holding the knife he'd used to kill his wife and her lover, and he'd been yelling and crying and claimed he didn't remember what had happened.

The mind had a way of blocking things out. Mrs. Moore must have dropped the knife next to her husband's body and kept going to get the mail as he'd intended to do, but she'd gotten confused and walked all the way to the sidewalk, forgotten what she was there for, and went back inside. The tech might find blood residue on the front doorknob or the jail matron might find a bloody tissue stuffed in the pocket of her housedress when they processed her, but there'd been no home invasion here. No third-party killer.

Love was as much a passion as jealousy and hate, and this clearly had been a crime of passion. Mrs. Moore had killed her husband out of love, the kind of love that lasted a lifetime.

Beecham closed the cabinet door and told the tech to bag the meds and take them into evidence. He walked through the living room, skirting the blood on the carpet. The body wagon had taken Mr. Moore away and now only the stain remained.

He glanced at a framed family photo on the wall next to the front door as he put on his overcoat. Records had identi-fied an adult daughter who still lived in Reno in one of the newer housing developments off the Mt. Rose Highway. In the photo she still looked happy.

The snow was coming down harder now. When he crossed

the street to his car, his footsteps crunched on ice that had been slush only a short time ago. He brushed the snow off his hair, then he sat inside his car while the defrosters did their bit and melted the frozen slush on the windows.

He could call in a favor and have the Reno cops do the next-of-kin notification, but Beecham felt he owed it to this couple to do the notification himself. It would take him a while to drive to south Reno given the weather, then he'd have to drive back to Sparks to do the formal interview with Mrs. Moore.

It was going to be a long night.

Before he put the car in drive, he turned on the car's MP3 player. He had it synced to his cell phone.

He pulled away from the curb to the sound of a Crosby, Stills & Nash song. It had been his aunt's favorite.

EYE OF THE NEWT

KEVIN J. ANDERSON

This volume would not be complete without a Dan Shamble story from New York Times *bestselling writer Kevin J. Anderson.*

Kevin has published more than 140 bestselling novels and with his wife, bestselling writer Rebecca Moesta, founded Wordfire Press eight years ago.

Kevin is known for Star Wars, X-Files, and Dune novels, as well as his many original science fiction novels. But back in 2012 he started something a little different for him, a series of humorous horror mysteries featuring Dan Shamble, Zombie P.I.

I love the fact that we have Dan Shamble in Pulphouse *Fiction* Magazine. *A Zombie Detective by the very nature of the concept belongs right here. A perfect Pulphouse idea.*

EYE OF THE NEWT

KEVIN J. ANDERSON

I

At Chambeaux & Deyer Investigations, even on quiet days, there's always paperwork to do, files to close out, dead cases to resurrect or just bury for good. I'm a detective—a zombie detective. I can throw a mean punch and stand up to the ugliest, foulest-smelling demon . . . but paperwork was never my forte. That's why I have an office assistant, Sheyenne. She's a ghost, and she's also my girlfriend. It doesn't matter that we intermingle our work lives and our personal lives, since neither of us is alive anyway.

Sheyenne had been re-alphabetizing files while I looked over cases I had recently wrapped up, some in more dramatic fashion than others, a few even verging on "end of the world" dramatic, so it's a good thing I'm skilled at my job. In studying the files, I wasn't looking for mistakes, just reviewing my greatest hits and wishing we had another case to work on at the moment.

My lawyer partner, Robin Deyer, was in court prosecuting a case of cemeterial fraud and incompetence—an underclass-action suit against a tombstone engraver who had committed far too many misspellings. Now that zombies were rising frequently from the grave, the formerly silent customers noticed the typos in their headstones, and a group had hired Robin to sue for damages on their behalf.

That left just Sheyenne and me in the offices. We had a dinner date planned for that evening, but we hadn't settled on a restaurant yet. It was mainly an excuse for us to be together, all form and no sustenance, since I rarely ate anyway and a ghost didn't eat at all.

In the meantime, as she flitted from one file cabinet to another, Sheyenne watched a small TV tuned to a local cable channel that covered the Stone Cold Monster Cookoff, which was taking place downtown in the Unnatural Quarter. A variety of skilled chefs competed in a days' long event; the crowds were getting larger now that the cookoff was down to three finalists. Sheyenne watched the unnatural chefs go about their extravagant preparations with enough pots, pans, and utensils to equip an inhuman army. She jotted down a recipe suggested by the loud, green-skinned Ragin' Cajun Mage, just in case she ever got around to cooking.

Then the office door crashed open, which was all the more remarkable because the creature that barged in was barely three feet tall. A scrawny lizard man with speckled brown skin, one yellow eye, and gauze and surgical tape covering where the other eye should have been.

"I need your help!" he said, in a phlegmy, hissy voice. "Are you, Dan Shamble? You've got to help me!"

"It's Chambeaux," I corrected him as I came out of my

office to greet him. I moved stiffly on joints that were still recovering from rigor mortis.

Sheyenne is usually very professional, but she cried out in delight when she saw him. "Oh, aren't you cute! Look, Beaux —he's from the car insurance commercials."

After stumbling inside, the lizard man slammed the door behind him with surprising strength. "That's a gecko," he snapped. His long tongue flicked in and out. "I'm a <u>newt</u>. There's a difference."

"Sorry if I offended you." She drifted forward to meet him. "Come in, sir. You're safe here."

I made sure my .38 was in its hip holster just in case the lizard man was being imminently pursued, but when no slavering eye-stealing monsters charged after him, I figured we had enough time for a normal client intake meeting. "Tell me what's going on, Mr., uh, Newt."

"My name is Geck." That must have been embarrassing for a guy who was too often confused for a humorous gecko insurance spokesman. "There's a hit out on me, and I was attacked last night."

"Who, exactly, is out to get you?"

He shook his head. "I don't know! I didn't think I had any enemies. I mean, I'm a warm and fuzzy guy . . . as far as an amphibian can be."

In the conference room I had to bring him a booster chair so he could see over the edge of the table. If Robin were here, she would have been taking copious notes on a yellow legal pad, but I just sat and listened. The one-eyed newt didn't seem at all bothered by the bullet hole in the center of my forehead, or my gray pallor. "Tell us your story, Geck."

He licked his lips. "I'm walking home, minding my own

business, whistling to myself, and then . . ." He shuddered. "Suddenly, I get accosted by two big thugs—a rock monster and a clay golem. 'Get him! He's the one we've got a contract out on,' says the rock monster, and the golem says, 'Don't end a sentence with a preposition.'

"And they grab me. Because it's a cool night, I'm a little lethargic. If I'd been sunning myself on a hot rock, I could've scurried out of their grasp, but I was too slow. They grab me, slam me up against the brick wall of an alley, then . . . they take out a long spoon." He shuddered again, sobbed. "They scoop out my eye, quick as you please, and pop it in a glass bottle. The golem holds me while the rock monster just laughs! 'We'd get twice as much if we took your other eye, too,' he says. 'You better watch yourself.' Then the golem says, 'He won't be watching much of anything now. Come on, we got what we need.'"

The newt self-consciously touched the wadded bandages on his face. "Then they went away and left me there. The golem seemed guilty, even sorry, but the rock monster was just mean."

"I'm not surprised," I said. "Rock monsters tend to be hard and grumbly, while golems are made of clay, so they are softer in general."

"What am I going to do?" Geck wailed. "If there's still a hit out on me, someone might try to take my other eye. I'm not safe."

I knew I could take him down to the precinct and ask for protective custody from my BHF, my Best Human Friend, Officer Toby McGoohan, but that would be only a temporary solution, and this needed more direct intervention.

"We have to find out who took out a contract on you," I

said. "Learn what you did, and try to make amends. Do you have *any idea* who it was? Who's got a grudge against you? Do you owe money?"

"Any idea at all?" Sheyenne pressed, hovering close to him.

Geck hung his head. He looked ill, although I knew the greenish-brown tinge to his hide was probably natural. "Only the library comes to mind. I think I've seen the rock monster and the golem there—they sometimes work as security guards. And I do have an overdue book and a fine." He blinked his remaining eye. "You don't think . . . ?"

Even Sheyenne paled, and I steeled myself. "You don't mess with the Spider Lady of the Unnatural Quarter Public Library. Everyone knows that." This was going to be a more dangerous case than I had expected. "We'd better go face her —in person, you and me, and see if we can resolve this. You won't be safe until you're off her hit list."

II

Geck and I headed through town toward the Unnatural Quarter Public Library main branch and Vault of Secrets. We made a side trip to his dank lair, a communal sub-basement where other newts shared the rent, with mud and moss for carpeting and a steady drip through the ceiling for running water. Not a good place to keep an overdue library book, I thought. At least he had it on a high shelf, away from the drip. Geck hauled over a stepstool so he could retrieve it.

"So, tell me about this book you checked out," I said. "How long is it overdue, and why is it so important?"

"A month overdue…I kept putting it off, Mr. Shamble. And then it got worse, and the fines built up." He held the thick volume close.

"How much?"

"Ten bucks."

"Better take twenty. We may need to pay off the Spider Lady, but we'll get you back on the straight and narrow."

He looked down at the heavy volume that seemed too big for him to carry. For the sake of efficiency, I took it from him, and we set off, while two other newts were waiting to stand under the ceiling drip for a shower.

"Never even finished it." Geck sounded guilty. "I went to the library for something to read in a puddle on a sunny day. I really enjoyed all the Harry Potter books, and I heard that the Harry Dresden novels by Jim Butcher were excellent, but they were all checked out.

"Then somebody said Shakespeare in the same sentence with Butcher, so I decided to look into that Shakespeare guy as my second choice. The only copy available was a rare special edition, <u>The Complete Pre-Humous Writings of William Shakespeare</u>. It was even autographed."

I frowned, knowing that someone who purported to be Shakespeare's ghost had been publishing new posthumously written plays and sonnets, but his claim had been debunked. He was, in fact, just another aspiring ghost writer with a good costume and literary airs, but apparently the library hadn't caught up yet.

"I tried to read the Shakespeare stuff, but I couldn't get into it," the newt said. "It wasn't like Harry Potter at all. It was boring. But I kept trying . . . and then the book was late, and I felt guilty, so I kept trying to read it. The fines piled up, and then I started getting threatening letters, so I was afraid to come to the library. And then . . ." He self-consciously touched the bandages covering his right eye."

"You need to bring the book back, and you'll have to make amends to the librarian," I said. "That may be the only way we can keep you intact, more or less. When we get to the library, let me do the talking. And bring your twenty bucks."

On our way across the Quarter, we passed vampires sitting outside under sun umbrellas at a blood bar. Two werewolf women offered discounts on "full claw treatment" pedicures. A mummy rode by on a bicycle, wobbling and unbalanced; he was taken completely off guard when one of his unraveled bandages caught in the chain, and he and the bicycle tumbled into the gutter.

We passed the Ghoul's Diner, where I often liked to sit at the counter with an abysmally bad cup of coffee and a disgusting miasma of a daily special. The diner and its unfortunate food were upstaged now, however, as the entire block had been barricaded off for the final rounds of the Stone Cold Monster Cookoff. A grandstand had been set up for the culinary acrobatics, and spectators gathered around, hoping for— or dreading—free samples.

I assumed the diner's business had suffered due to the event, but the ghoul proprietor never seemed to pay much attention to the outside world or his customers. It was business as usual.

In fact, everyone in the Unnatural Quarter—monsters and humans—got along about as well as anybody got along in the rest of the world. Ever since the Big Uneasy more than a decade ago, the world had been settling down from the change. The event had been caused by a strange alignment of planets and a completely coincidental spilling of virgin's blood on an original copy of the <u>Necronomicon</u>, which resulted in cosmic upheavals, rifts in the universal continuum, a shift in reality.

But after all that was over, naturals and unnaturals had to learn how to coexist, and everyday life returned with surprising stability. It could have been a real zombie apocalypse, but it wasn't so much an apocalypse as an awkward reunion.

Back then, I was a private investigator who hadn't seen much success in the real world, but I found a whole new clientele among the unnaturals. My business partner Robin joined me because she insisted that downtrodden unnaturals needed legal representation, too. Everything had been going fine— until one of my cases went south, and I ended up being shot in the back of the head.

These days, that isn't quite as final as it might sound. I rose from the grave and got right back on the case, eventually solving my own murder, then moving on.

It goes to show how much the world has settled into a new normal if a crowd of naturals and unnaturals can get excited about a cookoff championship.

Up on stage, after a round of digestive elimination, the Stone Cold culinary marathon had settled on its three finalists. On the left side of the grandstand was Leatherneck, a burly man in a leather apron, leather mask, and upright shocks of greasy hair. He used a rusty shovel to scoop mangled animal remains into the hopper of a meat grinder that was about the size of a wood chipper.

"To make Texas chainsaw chili," he said, "any sort of road kill will do—as long as it's been seasoned with hot sun and asphalt for at least four days."

The meat grinder whirred and spat out a brownish-red paste flecked with hair and fur that glopped into an already bubbling cauldron. The big chef added a pinch of salt, bent over to sniff the pot, then held up a gigantic razor-edged butcher knife. He raised his left forearm, which was a network of white scars. Without flinching, Leatherneck drew the blade down his forearm, opening up a wide gash that bled profusely into the pot. He held his arm over the chili as red dripped into the sauce, then with bright eyes behind his leather mask, he said, "And now for the special ingredient." The crowd fell into a hush, and the big man lifted up a jar of green spices with his non-bleeding arm. "<u>Oregano!</u>" He sprinkled a third of the jar into his pot.

The vampires in the audience had become extremely attentive when they watched him shed blood for his chili, but the oregano left them with sour frowns.

Next up was a heavyset, matronly woman whose beehive hair had a white lightning stripe, like the bride of Frankenstein. Her skin was chalky and pale, but her eyes were fiery red. Sheyenne sometimes watched her TV show, "Kitchen Litch," and she complained that the Kitchen Litch considered herself superior to her viewers. "The sort of person who would say 'tomaaahto coulis' instead of ketchup," Sheyenne had described her.

The Kitchen Litch held a large sauté pan over a gas burner. "Every ingredient must be frrrrresh," she said with an exaggerated roll of her r's. "First, we start with clarified butter." She ladled a greasy yellow pool into the pan, then reached inside a wicker basket, rummaging around. "And the frrreshest of frrresh is an ingredient that is . . . *alive!*"

She pulled out a black beetle as large as her hand. It squirmed and thrashed, but she threw it onto the sizzling pan. "And I always keep a special container of fresh blood-sucking gnats for garnish, but that will be for the finish." She reached into the basket to grab another beetle, while the first beetle flopped and hopped, dancing on the hot pan surface. Its black carapace cracked open, and it buzzed its wings to fly away.

"No, no!" The Kitchen Litch swatted with a spatula as the second skittering beetle also tried to take flight. She smashed that one into a pulp, and it sizzled in a little beetle patty in the frying pan. The first beetle, though, got away, winging up from the stage. Three more beetles escaped from the still-open wicker basket, and the flustered Kitchen Litch slammed the lid back down. Trying to recover her composure, she said to the audience, "Of course, frrresh ingredients also pose certain challenges." She busied herself nursing the beetle patty with her spatula.

The third chef, a loud green-skinned man, the Ragin' Cajun Mage, cooked flamboyantly beside two large glass aquariums filled with thrashing ingredients. He looked at the Kitchen Litch with scorn. "I agree with my incompetent rival—fresh ingredients are key, but so are *secret* ingredients, and I have about a dozen secret ingredients."

The Cajun Mage rapped his knuckles against the aquariums filled with silty gray-brown water. Swarms of thrashing tentacles writhed at him like a wrestling match between a squid and an octopus. Armored claws clacked in another aquarium. "We have a live mutant crawdad tank and a live assorted-tentacles tank. They'll wait, though, until my nightmare etouffee is ready. It takes half a day to simmer properly. First, we make a nice roux, starting with some perfect sassafras filé." He dumped a gray-green powder into the bottom of his stockpot. "Then some toadstool filé."

His eyes twinkled as he lifted up a crystalline vial. "And for the perfect seasoning, the tears of heartbroken girls. Two tablespoons will do." He poured the vial into the pot, then whisked it around as he increased the heat.

Geck and I had paused to watch the show. The smells wafting around the grandstand were an odd mix of appetizing and disgusting. My client glanced around the crowd, fidgeting and nervous, as if afraid someone might attack him right there out in the open, but I was sure he would be safe here. The Spider Lady from the library would not make a move on him at the Monster Cookoff. She had already delivered her ominous message.

One of the escaped black beetles buzzed through the air toward us, wobbling like a drunken bumblebee. Geck's yellow eye brightened, and he swiveled his salamander-like head, poised, tense . . . then he lashed out with his tongue. But he missed the beetle entirely, which buzzed away unaffected.

Geck groaned. "Bloody depth perception! I'm going to starve!"

As the green-skinned Cajun Mage moved to the next stage of his highly complex recipe, I nudged the newt along. "Come on, then. It's off to the library. This is a matter of life or death."

———

III

The Unnatural Quarter Public Library and Vault of Secrets was not meant to be a terrifying place, but Geck looked as if he would rather have been going to the dentist—and I didn't even know if newts had teeth.

The large stone building was impressive in one sense, looming in another sense. A poster in one of the dust-specked windows said "Come for fun in the library!" in blood-dripping letters. Because the stone steps were so widely spaced, I had to help Geck up each one.

As we climbed to the pillared entrance, he seemed more and more nervous. "You have to face this," I said. "If we can resolve your overdue library book, the Spider Lady will take you off her hit list, then you won't have to worry any more." The newt swallowed and moved on.

At the top of the broad steps, two fierce-looking stone lions crouched on pedestals. Just as we reached the top of the platform, a nervous-looking vampire scuttled out of the library entrance with a book hidden under his arm—and the two stone lions woke up. The ferocious living statues snorted, snarled, and rose on their heavy paws.

The nervous vampire clutched his book and scuttled backward, looking from side to side, trapped. One lion bounded off its pedestal and pinned him to the ground. He flailed and screamed. "I'll check out the book, I promise. I'll check it out!"

The vampire had been trying to smuggle out a hardcover copy of *Twilight*.

With a snort, the stone lion smacked the vampire and sent

him careening back into the library. Though uninjured, he was extremely embarrassed to have his reading material revealed.

The incident did little to calm Geck's nerves. I tried to reassure him, "I'm here to protect you and negotiate on your behalf." I did not point out that even the most highly skilled zombie P.I. could do little to protect against giant stone lions or demonic head librarians.

The main library smelled of books, that weighty, dusty aroma that always brings back nostalgic memories. The patrons included humans, particularly college students doing reports on the social changes brought on by the Big Uneasy. Mummy scholars worked with large stacks of papyrus, jotting down notes in hieroglyphics. Vampires developed family trees, while full-furred werewolves stood muttering together in the Pets section.

On the high shelves, accessible only by rickety ladders that looked more dangerous than the evil spell books themselves, a cleaning crew of goblins skittered about stringing cobwebs. In the middle of the floor, two large spinner racks held paperback bestsellers.

Geck looked around nervously, scanning the library. He whispered, "I don't see the rock monster or the golem. They're usually guarding the doors. Maybe they're off stealing someone else's eye."

"Or maybe it's their day off," I said.

"Or, maybe they're waiting to pounce on me again! Keep your eyes open, Mr. Shamble. You have more of them than I do."

At the main reference desk sat a withered, prim old woman who looked as if she suffered from chronic hemorrhoids. Her hair was pulled back into a bun so tight she didn't need a facelift, and she wore cat's-eye glasses that were large enough to be used as a weapon. She scanned the library like a high-tech targeting system, and when a young college couple began talking too loud, she suddenly reached out with a freakishly long, multi-jointed arm that held a ruler. Even though they were twenty feet away, she rapped on the table in front of them. "Quiet please in the library!" The old woman folded her extra arm back down under the desk.

Her nameplate said, "Hi, I'm Frieda. I'm here to help."

I nudged Geck, and we walked up to the desk. The newt was far too short, and I had to lift him up so he could meet the cat's-eye glasses with his remaining eye.

I looked behind the counter and saw that Frieda the Spider Lady had a nest of additional multi-jointed limbs all curled up beneath her flower-print dress. One set of hands was typing, while another paged through a printed book; behind her, two more limbs reached out to pluck volumes off a shelving cart. She gave us part of her attention. "How may I help you?"

"I'm Dan Chambeaux, Private Investigator, ma'am, and this newt is my client, Geck. I'm afraid there's been some misunderstanding, and I'm here to help resolve it."

The librarian frowned. "Misunderstanding? If words and sentences were stated clearly, there would be no misunder-standings."

"My library book is late," Geck blurted out, sounding ashamed.

The Spider Lady practically recoiled, as if he had hurled a terrible insult at her. "That changes things. Substantially."

I interjected, holding up the Shakespeare Pre-Humous Writings volume I had carried from his dank quarters. "My client has incurred library fines, which he is willing to pay, so long as he stops receiving threatening letters from the library. As you can see, he has already suffered a great deal of physical harm." I used my "be reasonable" voice, which rarely worked against villains; even so, the detective training handbook suggested being reasonable as a first step.

Frieda's voice was filled with venom. "And what is this book? How valuable is it?" Beneath the counter, her hidden limbs twitched. Many of them ended in claws. "And how despicable are you?"

Geck stammered and held out a rumpled receipt, while I slid over the book. The Spider Lady nudged her cat's-eye glasses, and her face seemed to wither even more. "This was part of our special Shakespeare collection—do you have any idea what sort of damage you've done? How many college treatises have been delayed because the authors had no access to this wonderful tome?"

"I . . . I'm sorry."

"And it's autographed too!" said Freda, as if that were the last nail in the coffin.

"You do realize that the autograph is fake, ma'am?" I pointed out, hoping tht might mitigate her ire. "The author of the posthumous works is not the real Shakespeare's ghost."

The librarian sniffed. "It's still of historical and popular interest." She shuffled papers and withdrew a formal parchment document that looked like a death-sentence decree. A dozen names were written on it, seven of which had been crossed off, as if terminated.

Geck the Newt was on the list, third from the bottom. "I'm sorry, I'm sorry!" he blubbered, then quickly slapped a moist and rumpled twenty on the counter next to her name plate.

"I'll pay the fine . . . I'll pay double!—just please don't send your goons after me. Don't take my other eye!"

Now it was the Spider Lady's turn to look off balance. "Take your other eye? Why on earth would I wish to do that? My sole reason for existence is to *encourage reading*. If I took your other eye, that would be against my principles, although the library does have a large selection of unabridged audiobooks."

I stood up for Geck. "My client was recently accosted in an alley by a rock monster and a golem, both of whom are known to work here in the library. If you didn't send them to steal his eye, then who did?"

The Spider Lady seemed flustered. "You must mean Rocky and Ned. They're just part-time contract security guards. It's so hard to find good security guards in the Unnatural Quarter —they tend to suffer unfortunate ends. But I had to let Rocky and Ned go. I caught them eating in the library, which is inexcusable."

She snatched the bill and used one folded arm to squirrel it away in a small cashbox, while another arm took the book and stacked it on the shelving cart behind her. With a third hand, she stamped PAID on her hit list next to Geck's name.

She reached out with another one of her long arms and slapped a zombie reader who had unconsciously folded down the corner of a page in order to mark his place. "Damage to library property! I *will* write you up."

I got her attention again. "If you didn't put out a contract to take my client's eye, then who did?"

"How should I know that?"

I indicated the sign on the desk. "It says you're a reference librarian."

"I'm afraid you'll have to do your own research, Mr. Shamble. You might begin by asking whether this action was a punitive measure against Geck specifically, or if someone actually needed the eye for some other purpose."

IV

I knew we could get worthwhile advice from the Unorthodox Lab Equipment and Organ Boutique, a small specialty business that catered to a broad clientele ranging from hobbyist mad scientists to evil corporate research centers with underground monster-development programs.

An imp named Gunther managed the place and kept all his wares in total disorganization on the shelves, like a secret code that only he knew how to interpret. His business had picked up dramatically after the demise of Tony Cralo's Body Parts Emporium, a giant organ superstore run by an obese zombie mobster. After I had exposed Cralo to justice, his business completely collapsed. Score one for the good guys. That annoyed many of the Quarter's mad scientists, however, because they could no longer do one-stop shopping.

The little imp was climbing a set of shelves and stacking glass jars filled with specimens preserved in formaldehyde. The jars themselves were as big as the diminutive imp, but he was strong. Gunther nearly lost his grip on a jar filled with intestines labeled with a sticker that said *Great for decorating!*

Seeing us, he swung down with simian agility and dropped with flat feet on the countertop. His gaze turned immediately toward the newt, focusing on the bandages.

"Looks like somebody's in the market for a new eye! I have a wide selection." He clucked his pointed tongue. "I'll have to take socket measurements, though. Would you like to match the original color, or should we try something more fashionable?"

Geck said, "I'd rather have my own eye back—and I want to keep the one I still have."

When I explained how my client had been attacked, the imp proprietor seemed very disturbed. "The Unnatural Quarter is going down the tubes. Sure, people used to get roofies and wake up in hotel bathtubs missing a kidney or two, but that was just an expected part of the business. Taking an eye right out on the streets?" The imp shook his head in disgust.

"Have you had any customers asking for an eye of newt?" I asked.

"Not in particular. Sure, newt eyes are rare, but I have a selection of perfectly adequate toad eyes and salamander eyes. They'll do in a pinch." He clucked his pointed tongue again, touching Geck's bandages. "I could make do, find something that'll fit you, though it might look a little odd. Any decent scientist could install one, so long as it's in good condition."

"But is there a reason why someone would particularly want Geck's eye?" I asked. "What are newt eyes used for?"

"I used mine for seeing," Geck snapped.

"I meant what would someone else use it for."

The imp pondered. "Various organs have potent sorcerous aspects, particularly the organs of magical creatures. Livers, spleens, pituitary glands, testicles, and the like. Rare, ancient magic books listed eye of newt as a vital ingredient for every sorceror to have in the pantry, but it was never used to work

112

magic. Those tomes weren't spell books." Gunther gave an impish grin. "They were recipes, you see."

"Recipes?" Wheels began to turn in my mind.

"Yes," said the imp. "Eye of newt is primarily used in cooking."

V

With a sinking feeling in the pit of my stomach, like the aftereffects of a bad pepperoni pizza, I hurried with the newt back to the Unnatural Quarter's Stone Cold Monster Cookoff.

We bumped into Officer Toby McGoohan, who was walking the beat and presumably maintaining order. The only orders, though, were being taken by shuffling zombie waitresses at the outside tables of the Ghoul's Diner.

"Hey, Shamble!" McGoo tipped his blue patrolman's cap. "Just another day on the job. There've been reports of culinary unrest." He nodded toward the grandstand where the three finalist chefs were finishing their hours-long preparations for their masterpiece dishes. Runners dispersed small samples among the spectators, who would then vote on the winner. No doubt there was illicit gambling, bookies taking bets as well as exchanging family recipes.

"If the wrong person wins, McGoo, there'll be some digestive upset among the crowd."

I noticed he was eating something wrapped in dripping

paper, a meal from one of the food carts that catered to the human audience members: a hot dog that was wrapped in bacon and stuffed inside a glazed jelly donut. McGoo took a bite, then frowned at the show on stage. "I don't know how anybody can eat that stuff." He wiped the congealing mess from his lips.

"We already have enough to make our stomachs queasy, McGoo. A couple of thugs roughed up my client, Mr. Geck. They took his eye last night. At first we thought it was payback for an overdue library book, a contract taken out on him by the Spider Lady herself."

McGoo paled, which made the freckles on his cheeks seem more prominent. "The Spider Lady?"

I held up a hand. "But it wasn't that. We think these thugs stole Geck's eye . . . for some nefarious purpose."

"There's always some nefarious purpose. Did you get a description of the perps?"

"Just general details. One's a rock monster, the other's a golem. Names are Ned and Rocky."

"That's enough to go on." McGoo pursed his lips. "I've been patrolling the crowd here. Lots of spectators, but I think I noticed that rock monster . . . now that you mention it, he was with a golem. They were sitting at one of the outdoor tables at the Ghoul's Diner. I only noticed them because the rock monster was eating a bagel—a toasted onion bagel, but with strawberry cream cheese on it." He frowned. "That's the sort of thing an attentive cop will notice."

To the roar of the crowd, Leatherneck ladled out samples of his Texas chainsaw chili, passing small cups around the crowd. He had reopened the big gash on his forearm so he could spruce up each bowl with a splash of blood. The vampire spectators crowded forward, eager to get their sample even with the addition of oregano to the pot. The persistent Kitchen Litch had managed to fricassee enough of the large beetles that she was prepared to serve, though she had not yet garnished the meal with her bloodsucking gnats.

The three of us hurried off to the diner at the edge of the cookoff crowd. Albert Gould had set up rickety card tables and temporary benches to take advantage of the additional customers, even though they were all watching the cookoff. McGoo pointed, "There's the bagel!"

I did see the onion bagel covered with strawberry cream cheese—which was certainly out of the ordinary—being held by a lumpy rock monster, a creature composed of assembled stones and a large yawning mouth just made to pulverize bagels. Next to him sat a gray clay golem sipping a tiny cup of espresso. I was shocked because I hadn't known the Ghoul's Diner served espresso.

Geck hopped up and down, trying to see. "That's them!"

On the stage with his big booming laugh, the green-skinned Ragin' Cajun Mage stirred his cauldron of nightmare etouffee. "Almost finished! Enjoy those other morsels while you can—and be prepared to surrender your taste buds to the Mage."

McGoo and I stepped up to the table, interrupting the rock monster and the golem. I tried to be as tough and determined as a zombie detective can be. "Are you Rocky? We'd like to have a word with you."

The rock monster turned its blocky head so I could see blazing red eyes deep within cave-like sockets. "I'm Ned. He's Rocky." He gestured to the golem, then took another big grinding bite of his bagel.

"We need to talk with both of you," I said.

McGoo puffed up his chest. "We've heard reports that you assaulted a citizen of the Quarter."

"Me, me!" said Geck, bouncing up and down. The newt was so short he didn't come up to the edge of the table, and the two thugs hadn't noticed him. I gave him a hand, lifting him up so the two could see him. "You stole my eye!"

"You got proof of that?" grumbled the rock monster. "It was dark in that alley. How can you be sure it was us?"

"So, you admit you were there," McGoo said.

Rocky the golem said, "Considering this person's condition, he's unreliable as an eye-witness."

Ned the rock monster snickered.

"It was them!" Geck said. "I'd point them out in a line-up any day of the week."

The rock monster rose to his feet, towering over us. "We took a job, we got paid. We're just blue collar workers."

Rocky stood up to join him. "A golem is required to follow whatever commands a master issues, even a temporary master. There's been a legal precedent. We're not responsible for whatever we allegedly did or didn't do."

Ned added, "Besides, five bucks is five bucks."

"And assault on a newt is still considered assault," said McGoo. "I'm going to have to—"

Geck suddenly cried out as he jumped onto the table, disturbing the tiny cup of espresso and knocking the half-eaten bagel to the ground. "Look, look! That's my eye!"

On stage, the Ragin' Cajun Mage stood over his noisome vat of nightmare etouffee. He tried to impart a sense of awe on the spectators. "And the last, the rarest, the most special secret ingredient—not available at stores!—we add for the finish, eye of newt!"

The crowd gasped.

Geck shrieked.

The green-skinned Cajun chef dangled the vial containing the stolen amphibian eye and let the silence hang for a long and dangerous moment. Even the large aquariums of live mutated crawdads and live assorted tentacles thrashed and churned, either applauding or dreading the imminent moment when they would become part of the cooking performance.

"That's my eye!" Geck yelled again and bounded toward the stage.

The crowd stopped munching on their fricasseed beetle samples or Texas chainsaw chili. Many dropped their cups on the ground.

McGoo withdrew his service revolver and pointed it at the Ragin' Cajun Mage. "Stop right there! That eyeball is private property. Everyone else, stay calm."

Of course the spectators panicked.

Knowing the crowd could turn ugly—well, the crowd was already ugly, but it could get worse—I pointed at the golem and the rock monster. They were both mercenaries to the core. "Five bucks if you help us resolve this," I offered.

"Each?" asked Ned.

I hesitated only a second and considered it a worthwhile investment. "Each."

The two large gray forms lumbered into the crowd.

The newt dashed up onto the stage with the speed of a sun-warmed lizard. Geck threw himself with a full fury at the Cajun Mage, attempting to tackle him and seize his eye before it fell into the cauldron of etouffee. Alas, unaccustomed to his lack of depth perception, Geck missed. He only brushed against the green-skinned cook and instead careened into the live aquariums, which the Mage chef had opened, preparatory to serving. Both glass cases toppled over, dumping out a menagerie of edible horrors. Hundreds of mutated crawdads and assorted live tentacles went thrashing into the crowd. People began screaming.

McGoo yelled, "Watch out! The ingredients are loose."

Tentacles flung themselves on fleeing mummies. Crawfish clipped their pincers on the spiky fur of a punk rocker were-wolf, who clawed his own cheeks in an attempt to get them off.

The Kitchen Litch quickly evacuated from the grandstand, taking the last samples of fricasseed beetles with her, but in her alarm, she bumped the sealed container of frrresh live blood-sucking gnats that she had reserved for garnish, and the swarm of black biting things flew up, indiscriminately buzzing around everyone on the stage.

Next to the cauldron, the Cajun Mage flailed, trying to beat back the frenzied one-eyed newt.

Rocky and Ned cleared a way through the crowd with all the finesse of two bulldozers, knocking people aside on their way to the stage. I followed them.

Ned bellowed at the chef in his cavernous voice, "We're going to need that eye back!"

"I'm going to need it!" Geck jumped up and down, grabbing for the vial clenched in the Mage's green hand.

More large black beetles had escaped from the Kitchen Litch's wicker basket, and Leatherneck, seemingly unphased by the chaos, reached out with his big strangler's hands and grabbed them to add to his pot of chainsaw chili.

McGoo stomped on the assorted tentacles and kicked away crawdads that nipped at his ankles. "Keep calm!" he yelled.

The golem and the rock monster got themselves so entangled in the rebellious ingredients that I made it to the stage first. The cloud of blood-sucking gnats swarmed around me, but the biting creatures went away disappointed, with no taste for embalming fluid.

The Cajun Mage looked indignantly into his etouffee. "But this would have been the perfect batch. You've ruined everything!" He dodged the newt and opened the glass vial. "Without the secret ingredient, it might as well just be a casserole. I must finish for the sake of the culinary arts!" He upended the vial over the cauldron.

As if in slow motion, Geck groaned, "Nooooo!"

But I got there just in time, lashing out with my outstretched hand. I caught the detached eye of newt in my palm, and it plopped there, sitting moist and squishy, unpleasant to the touch . . . but safe.

Rocky and Ned reached the stage just as I backed away cradling Geck's eye. The golem and the rock monster grabbed the Cajun Mage, lifted him up, and dumped him into the large pot of nightmare etouffee, where he stirred and whisked himself helplessly.

Geck hurried over to me, trembling. "You saved my eye! Do you think it can be reattached?"

"There's a good chance. We have the best mad scientists in the Quarter," I said. "Though, from now on, you may need reading glasses."

Rocky the golem loomed over me. "That'll be five bucks."

"Each," said Ned.

I carefully handed the jiggly eye to Geck's loving care,

while I dug in my wallet. By now, most of the crowd had run screaming and the loose ingredients had dispersed.

The Kitchen Litch had run away, plagued by vengeful beetles, and the only one remaining on the stand was burly Leatherneck, who calmly ate his chili straight from the ladle. "Last chef standing. I guess that means I win."

McGoo handcuffed the thoroughly etouffeed Cajun chef, who was still trapped inside his cauldron, although out of courtesy he turned the heat down to a slow simmer. The Ragin' Cajun Mage struggled to lift a gooped finger to his lips, tasted it, "After all that, it still could use salt."

I called Sheyenne back at the office and asked her to look up the best eyeball replacers in the Quarter. I suggested that Gunther the imp might be able to give a recommendation.

Out in the wreckage in front of the grandstand, I saw Albert and two of his waitresses running around with shovels and five gallon buckets, scooping up the dropped samples of Texas chainsaw chili and fricasseed beetles. I could guess what might be on tomorrow's special board for the Ghoul's Diner.

Leaving McGoo to take care of the arrested chef, I led Geck back toward my offices. I recalled that I had promised to take Sheyenne out for a dinner date, but I realized I didn't have much appetite.

Maybe we would go dancing instead.

LIFETIME VALUE

B.A. PAUL

In B.A. Paul's second original story in Pulphouse, just as she did with the first story, gives us one of the most memorable characters I have seen in a long time...

But the character is not a third-floor girl.

Another amazingly memorable story and character I can't say too much about for fear of ruining the story for you.

For some free short stories and a lot more about her work, do make time to check out her web site at https://www.bapaul.com/

LIFETIME VALUE

B.A. PAUL

I 'm good at what I do. That's why he chose me.

I close the green leather-bound ledger and lean back in the wooden office chair. One of those old-time designs. Heavy oak, swivel base, casters. Armrests permanently set at an unnatural height.

Mini rectangles of light illuminate the dark wood paneling along one wall, but the rays only make it two-thirds of the way down on a sunny day. Most days aren't sunny. I can see the occasional pair of feet walking by on the sidewalk above. Some heels clacking. Some tennis shoes pounding. Strolling or hurrying off to their destinations.

None the wiser of the goings-on here.

I reach for the metal lamp and twist the switch at the top of the shade. The heat from the bulb radiates through the scuffed black paint, burning my fingertips. I've been working a while.

Likewise for the black oscillating fan sitting on the massive desk opposite the lamp—the switch is hot, a complaint from spinning too long. Another relic. Metal blades. A near-frayed electrical cord that would send OSHA running for their clip-boards and violation forms—if they knew. The kind of fan that would fetch pretty pennies at auction, money handed over by yuppies to decorate their apartments in things gone by.

Art deco, I think they call it. But that's not my area, décor.

I'm a book person. Numbers. Figures. I run my hand over the ledger and my heart sinks because I know what information lurks in those gold-gilded pages. I know every name. I've committed to memory every dollar sign and date. I'll need that information.

And I'll need it soon.

I stand and stretch, and my neck and lower back give satisfying pops. I really have been sitting here for quite some time. I glance at the wall opposite the desk at the round clock as I reach back for my ponytail and twist it into a tight bun on the top of my head. The clock has a white face, black numbers. Old school, hard-wired into the electric. Red second hand tumbling around and around in jerky rhythm. When all is quiet and the fan blades are still, I can hear the clock's hum.

I walk across the room and make sure everything is just how he likes it.

The room is just so. He'll be pleased with the work I've accomplished.

If I didn't know any better, if I were watching myself on a screen from some other vantage point than the doorway of this undergrown den, I'd think this was a setting from one of those old detective movies. Antique and eclectic. Dusty and hazy. Right down to the office door with the frosted glass panel window inset. Fading white letters. OFFICE.

If I didn't know any better.

———

My dorm is on the fourth floor. I take the stairs up after locking the office. Steps worn with age, ever so slightly dented in the middles where the marble has given up after decades of foot traffic. I've taken to using the very sides of the steps. Where the angles are sharp, level. And where the marble still holds its original cut. I can move faster that way without fear of planting a foot awkwardly on one of those wavier steps.

So many trips up and down from the dorm. To the office. To the girls' hall.

I've cataloged all my movements and the locations of the waviest steps in my head as if they were an entry in the green ledger. Intimately familiar.

I round the landings on floors One and Two, which are quiet, then keep to the right as I scale another level. From the girls' hall on Three, giggles sneak under the closed metal fire doors. I pause for a moment on Three's landing. I'm not out of breath from the climb—I climb up and down these stairs all day. Every day. Doing his bidding.

Quite the contrary. My strength is at its peak.

No. I catch my breath because the giggles are misguided. Giggles over their new-found gifts. And they'll be happy playing dress up in new clothes and doing one another's nails in all shades of pinks and crimsons. Pulling blonde hair into sparkling barrettes and taming brunette curls with glittering headbands. Painting faces with the highest-quality makeup money can buy.

I know what gifts they've received. Every evening gown,

right down to the maker and size for each of the sixteen girls. Every "spa day kit."

Because I bought those items. I hung the spa supplies, tucked into red satin drawstring bags, from each door's knob last night. I hung each evening gown from the ornate brass hooks he'd installed above and to the right of each door frame. So the gowns wouldn't wrinkle.

Because it's Auction Night. And the giggles will soon be stifled.

And I know this because this is my fourth Auction Night with him.

And I'm good at what I do.

And because this time, I know one of the sixteen from before. From before I was Melanie Hampshire.

I stand and listen as the laughter and surprised gasps die down, the girls retreating into their rooms to get ready for the big event. I reach out and touch the metal door, cold and stark gray, but I dare not enter their hall. Not yet.

I scale the remaining flight and open my set of metal doors on Four. My room is across from his. When he's here. And today, he's here. I see light spilling into the hallway and the shadows of movement as feet break the rays' path from under the door.

I turn to my dorm and open the door. It's never locked. I only need a key for the office.

And a set of keys for the rooms on Three.

I close the door behind me and lean on it. Not from fatigue or weariness—even though I've gotten little sleep over the last few nights. Preparing. Shopping. Keeping the books. I lean and breathe deeply because it's almost done.

When he'd chosen me, I thought I'd live on the third floor,

but I didn't make that cut. After I saw the girls that did, I understood why. They are impeccable. Flawless. So perfect that in all actuality, the makeup I'd placed in some of their bags could have the opposite effect—toning down their beauty instead of accentuating it.

Me, not quite so much. I'm not bad looking. I was deemed worthy of the other position. Of his trusted—almost trusted—right-hand dorm room supervisor. He'd done his research. He'd found the information on me that I'd wanted him to find.

Melanie Hampshire. Near photographic memory. Quiet. Unattached with no family. Minimal social media footprint.

No one would miss Melanie. No one would miss me.

I went to the kitchenette and poured a glass of ice water and sat on the stool at the counter. The only stool, chrome legs and trim. Padded vinyl yellow seat in need of patching. I spin the glass on the counter and watch as condensation begins to form. I try to zone out, but it doesn't work.

I can't because I know what's happening under my feet one floor down.

At first, he had me placing signs all over the city. Professionally made advertisements for his modeling agency. A real, true-to-life agency. Complete with legal bookkeeping and portfolios and reviews from girls young and old. Boys young and old, too.

I take a sip and feel the cool water snake down to my stomach. I trace the sweaty tears on the glass. And then I turn from the tiny kitchenette to face the far wall of my dorm where my twin bed sits across from a mahogany armoire.

When I was a kid, I loved reading the Narnia books. Now, after 492 days of living in the dorm, I never want to see—or read about—any armoire ever again.

I approach the piece and swing open the door. It's taller than I am, and the space for the hanging clothes takes up half of the interior's width. The other half is filled with pull-out drawers with knobs in the shape of roses. Etched vines and leaves wiggle over the drawer fronts and on the doors and trim. I've traced them. Memorized them, as well.

He's left me a gift inside the armoire. One that he picked out. One that I'm to wear tonight while I keep his gold-gilded ledger down to the very last decimal point.

A simple black gown. Straight cut down to the hip area where it flares just a bit. A rim of dainty rhinestones trims the waist area. Elegant enough to stand by his side, but understated. As to not draw attention one way or the other from the main attractions.

From one of the rose knobs hangs a black satin choker with a single clear stone. In the closet, three more black gowns hang in silent tribute, all different cuts. One strapless. One spaghetti. One off-shoulder. Worn once each. I'd draped the chokers and necklaces for those evenings around the hangers and stored them with the gowns.

You'd think I would push the gowns as far back in the armoire as they could go. But I don't. They remind me that I'm here for a reason. That patience pays off. That diligence poured into every detail of this place, of him, of the girls, is not in vain.

The three black dresses remind me that I'm good at what I do.

Those three nights I count as losses. Three auctions. Fifty girls. Girls come and now gone. Girls dreaming of being molded into masterpieces at his hand. The Third Floor girls. How much better they were than the ones simply taking sessions on the Second Floor, simple headshots in the studios or three-pages portfolios for some other agency. The *Third Floor* girls are the ones that have his promise that *they* have promise. And potential.

And what a grand amount of money they will make over their lifetimes with their flawlessness. What a lavish lifestyle they'll enjoy. He promised.

And their lifetime value would just increase and increase...

I lay the gown on my bed and smooth the fabric. I retrieve the choker and open the single window above my futon. Outside my window there's a rusty fire escape that barely clings to the side of the building and drops into the alley below. But he knows I won't leave. I brush my hand over my left hip where the tracker sends him updates of my whereabouts.

I don't go anywhere where he doesn't know. Sometimes I sit with my right leg out of the window, dangling in freedom, while the left leg stays firmly inside the dorm room.

The girls under me don't need trackers. The allure of lavishness is enough to keep them chained.

He didn't know when he'd chosen me that I didn't need a tracker either. That I'd chosen him first. And I'm here to stay.

I reach outside the window where I'd loosened a nail from the wooden casing. I hang the choker there, on the rusty nail. And I dangle my right leg out and pray.

———————

I shower, and while in the bathroom I can hear the rattle of the fire escape, but I dare not go toward the window. To see who came. To see a familiar face from my life before.

From before I was Melanie Hampshire.

My heart beats faster, and I will myself to calm. Thousands of trips up and down the marble staircase. Countless nights of sleepless planning. Hundreds of hours of prep.

All leading up to this night.

I dress in the gift he left. He has a way with sizes. The gown is a perfect fit. I return to the bathroom and blow dry my hair. Plain brown hair, somewhat frizzy. I trim a few frayed ends over the commode. I pull the locks up and into a tight bun and secure it with a rhinestone-tipped clip.

Makeup is next. To cover the freckles and fill in the tiny lines. More lines now than a year ago. Lines etched by extreme concentration on the ledger. On the building.

On him.

The freckles and the plainness. Why I'm not a Third Floor girl.

Satisfied with the image and brown eyes staring back at me, I leave the mirror and walk to the window, still open.

I reach out and feel for the choker. I remove it from its hanging spot and close the window. The breeze is a bit cooler now than it was an hour ago.

I go to the nightstand by my bed and turn on the switch. A lamp, black metal, similar but smaller than the one in the office. I hold the choker under the light. I see no flaws save a minuscule nick near a prong that holds the rhinestone—and now the microphone—in place.

Someone else on my team is good at what they do, too.

I unhook the clasp and wrap the piece around my neck and hook it in place. I go back to the mirror to examine the finished product. I can't see the nick when it's on my neck. I hope he won't be able to, either.

I slip into my black heels, glad that I'll be using the elevator this evening. Hoping I won't need the memorized map of stairs in the building. I step into the hallway and turn to face the dorm that's been my home for 492 days. The twin bed. Made with military corners. The futon. Rarely sat upon. Never unfolded. The kitchenette. Wiped and sanitized.

The window. My saving grace.

And I pull the door shut.

————

He meets me in the hallway and we walk to the elevator. He puts in his key and I step into the car with him. The silver doors slide shut. He examines my dress. My hair. He adjusts the rhinestone on my throat and I hold my breath for a millisecond. Then he smiles and nods.

I've passed the test.

We slip through the belly of the building down to the office. I wait in the elevator while he opens the office door and retrieves his ledger from the desk. Right where I'd left it. He joins me, slides his key into a different lock, and we ride up to the first floor. When *No. 1* lights up above our heads and the door slides open, we're in a new world.

The bustle of cocktail hour with tuxedoed waiters balancing silver trays of champagne and hors d' oeuvres is such a contrast to the Third Floor. And the photography studios on Second. It took my breath away the first time I saw it. And it takes my breath tonight.

He smiles and leads me through the fray of bodies and music and food to a room off the main ballroom. Rows of chairs covered in red velvet wait for their audience. A stack of bidding paddles waits on a table in the back. White. Round. With black numbers and smooth wooden handles.

He takes me and the ledger to the front podium. I open the book and turn to tonight's offerings.

Sixteen names.

Sixteen girls.

Sixteen "someone's daughters," all with their LV columns filled in.

And organized from lowest to highest lifetime value.

Whether used as models or call girls or sold some other way is none of his concern. Or mine—so I'm told. Every name in the ledger has a running total of monies spent for room, board, evening gowns, and photo shoots. But the LV column is most important for Auction Night. That's why the buyers come.

They want to bid on the girl with the highest possible lifetime value. He uses a top-secret set of calculations, developed by him, on every girl ever to come through the door. Those calculations determine whether a pretty face will be a Third Floor girl or simply get the standard package from the photography front of the Second Floor.

He used the calculation on me. He told me my LV was unimportant because I was good at what I did. He was to keep me. Indefinitely.

I take my seat in one of the three chairs on the stage as he retrieves the gavel and block set from the podium's cabinet. He positions them just so next to the ledger. I glance to my right. A doorway there leads to the elevator's hall. Where the girls will bypass the festivities in the ballroom and take a seat in one of the sixteen chairs that line the wall. Spotlights shine on these seats. Their rhinestones and glitter will sparkle and shine, hopefully catching the eye of someone with money.

Lots of money.

Four times I've been on this stage. Four auctions. Three down. One about to go. And the weight of the rhinestone's microphone presses the air out of my lungs.

————————

The girls are seated in a line of sixteen. The one I know from before looks straight ahead. She's good at what she does, too.

Some would call us a team. Him and me. And the sixteen girls.

But the real team is her, me, and the unknown tech guru from my fire escape.

I'd chosen a choker similar to mine from the jewelry inventory for her. One with a stone and setting large enough for tech. I slipped it into her red satin drawstring kit, the one I'd placed outside her door last night in preparation for Auction Night. And I knew from before I was Melanie that there would be a nail, rusted or not I don't know, protruding from a Third Floor window casing. Just over the fire escape.

This girl. She lived directly under my feet.

I don't look at her now, except when I scan the entire row of young ladies, giving each of them the exact same count of attention so as not to draw attention. The glances understated as always. She crosses her left leg over her right and tucks them under her chair.

She's ready.

The third auction, the one that we'd missed on, the familiar face in the line of girls—a different face from this evening—had given the same signal, but something had gone wrong. And the auction went forward.

Major loss. I don't know what happened to the undercover girl. I only know her Lifetime Value number. It was high. She was sold.

He stands at the podium and adjusts the gooseneck on the microphone for his height. Tall. Muscular. Handsome. No aspiring model would say no to him. To his offers.

I'd asked him after the second auction why he insists on doing the auction himself. Why risk being seen when he usually stays in the background of the top two floors. And I'm the face in front of the ladies and the go-between.

He gave a charming grin and said Auction Night is his pet. His creation. And that demanded he be seen and remembered. To grow the business.

And that he trusted only me to keep careful care of the business and the girls in between the auctions because I was, well, forgettable.

And he'd put this in such a way that I almost took it as a compliment.

Almost.

I look to my right and scan the row of girls as the audience, bidders and their business cohorts, fill the red cushioned seats. Many have paddles. Some are drunk. Realization hits a few of the young women. But I bought them high-end makeup so the mascara doesn't smear when the tears start. Sparkling tears to match their glitter and stones.

The familiar face does well, blending in. Pretending to have just caught on to something that she's known for as long as I have. She wraps one arm around the midsection of her red evening gown. She brings her other hand up and rests it on her shoulder. I know she does this to move her fingers that much closer to the rhinestone choker. Others assume she's self-comforting in the realization of her fate. She blends in well. Even in glittering scarlet.

The seats are filled with eager bodies. He stands behind the podium, raises the hammer, then brings it down hard on the block. The audience startles and hushes. The girl in the turquoise gown can't stifle her sob, but she's ignored by the horde. The girls on either side of her dare not move to comfort her.

He welcomes his guests. He ignores the merchandise. Treats them as such. As if they're inanimate objects. Which brings more sobbing. Because until today, he'd treated each one as if she were the only girl in the universe. Someone with value. Personal value to him.

He gives introductory rules, reminds them all of the contracts they'd signed before arriving, and begins the bidding.

My familiar lady in red glances in my direction and I catch this out of the corner of my eye. We allow the first girl in line to be sold. A relatively low LV, and she went quickly. Everyone's waiting for the higher values to come to the block.

The girls remain seated until the end when their owners will gather them and escort them out of the building. Never to be Third Floor girls again.

We allow the second girl's auction to proceed. A little more money changes hands. As he brings the gavel down and pronounces "sold," I see my teammate tap her choker.

Please work this time.

The third and fourth girls are sold.

He reads out loud the fifth's description. He highlights height, weight. Natural hair color. Eye color. Maintenance costs. And as he is about to disclose her LV figure to the audience, the back doors burst open.

And just like that, Auction Night is over.

———

I allow myself to be cuffed. As does she.

Others go with more of a tussle. Upstanding businessmen outed. Fathers found out. Someone's brother. Someone else's husband. A couple of wives. There are too many for metal cuffs. Some of them now wear standard black zip ties as they leave the building.

And he. He is to be free no more. A prisoner of his own making in a prison made by others. And certainly much less comfortable than the dorms of Third Floor.

In the squad car, the officer unlocks the cuffs. I gaze at the stars through the window. Sparkling like rhinestones. I reach up and let down my hair, relaxing a bit. I make sure they bring the ledger. I take off the choker. My hidden microphone captured enough of the auction to be proof. But the ledger was the real evidence.

And the testimonies of the fifteen young ladies we'd saved. Impeccable women. Flawless. Unforgettable.

And as I wait for the ride to the station, back to my life before I was Melanie Hampshire, I wonder where the other girls are. Likely no longer flawless or impeccable. I remember the three black dresses hanging in my armoire. Three auctions' worth of girls. Gone.

But I know all of their names. All the girls lost in the two information-gathering auctions. And the auction we blew. I know their vital statistics. Height, weight. Eye and hair color. I know their values. Their true values, not the digits and decimals in the LV column of the green ledger.

He'd told me I was forgettable.

But I haven't forgotten any of them.

I'm good at what I do.

HEY, DIDDLE, DIDDLE

CHRISTINA F. YORK

It is stunning to me that this was only Christina F. York's second story in Pulphouse. *Chris has helped me out with this magazine since the mailing parties with the first incarnation. In fact, she organized them.*

And as a writer, under lots of names, she has written many cozy mystery novels both for traditional publishers and indie, as well as a number of Star Trek stories for me back when I was editing Star Trek: Strange New Worlds *for ten years.*

Chris's most recent cozy mystery novel is just out. To find out more about her work and her many mystery names, go to www.york-writers.com

HEY, DIDDLE, DIDDLE

CHRISTINA F. YORK

Alphonse listened to the track announcer calling the end of the Meadowland Stakes race, as he watched from the rail. The thunder of hooves shook the ground under his feet, and dust assailed his nose, as the racers passed his position.

Fairy Dust was one of his favorites, even though trainers weren't supposed to have favorites.

And Bubbles, the jockey, was one of his favorites, too. He probably shouldn't have favorite jockeys, either, but screw that. She looked good in the silks, and he could imagine what she would look like out of them. Hell, he'd even had a preview or two in the changing rooms, even though the women's locker was supposed to be off limits to men.

But Bubbles didn't feature having him in her life, not by a long shot. Not as long as she was a unicorn racer. Just his luck to fall for a woman with a career that didn't leave much room for romance.

It wasn't like he hadn't tried. He'd done all the polite things, made all the non-threatening moves he knew.

Both of them.

But she'd been pretty clear. He couldn't find a good answer to "Get your damned hands off of me." She might be little, but dainty wasn't a word that described Bubbles.

Fairy Dust was moving along the rail, challenging for the lead, with only a few seconds left in the race. He seemed to respond to the screaming of the crowd, putting on a last-second burst of speed, and moving into a photo finish.

While the crowd buzzed, waiting for the results, Alphonse slipped through the gate into the paddock, where the mounts were cooling down.

As a trainer, he was one of the few people allowed near the unicorns. Only virgins could ride, but fortunately trainers didn't have to be quite so pure. He'd thought about being a jockey once, but that whole no-sex-thing had changed his mind. Who wanted to voluntarily spend the rest of his life in a constant state of frustration?

Bubbles was still astride *Fairy Dust*, leaning forward over his neck, stroking his horn, and whispering in his ear.

Alphonse suddenly wished he was a unicorn.

As she stroked the horn, Bubbles stood up slightly in her saddle, leaning forward. The tight silk of her riding pants stretched across her trim bottom.

Was the woman deliberately torturing him?

Bubbles glanced around the paddock, catching sight of Alphonse. Her eyes were bright with the excitement of the race, and a little unfocused, her face flushed. She smiled at Alphonse, and nudged *Fairy Dust* toward him.

Sliding from the saddle, Bubbles dropped down next to Alphonse. "Did you see the son-of-a-bitch run?" She was buzzing with adrenaline. "Did you <u>see</u>?"

Before Alphonse could reply, the finish photo flashed on the tote board. *Fairy Dust*, muscles straining, had pushed his horn ahead of the number two finisher, by a fraction of an inch.

Bubbles cheered, and jumped into Alphonse's arms, wrapping her slender legs around his waist, and kissing him lustily.

For an instant, they were both in the moment, in the kiss, passion and desire flowing freely.

Then Bubbles broke the kiss and dropped to the ground. Her face clouded, and frustration instantly replaced passion.

"Dammit!" She stomped away. "Don't do that to me!"

As she moved off, Alphonse could hear a string of muttered curses. He shook his head.

She was trying to torture him.

———

The jockey's changing room was a miasma of steam and sweat, the clash of a dozen different soap and shampoo scents creating a stomach-churning cloud of olfactory overload.

Bubbles shoved her way to her locker, shooting dirty looks at anyone who crossed her part.

"Watch out," called a tiny woman wrapped in a towel. "Bubbles is horny. Again!"

"Am not!" Bubbles shot back.

The retort was greeted with a wave of laughter from all over the room.

"You sooo are too," the woman replied. She stopped in front of a locker with the name "Rainbow" stenciled on the front, and pulled out a small silver flask. "Here," she tossed it to Bubbles, "drown your sorrows."

Bubbles tilted her head back and took a long swallow from the flask before tossing it back to Rainbow. "I don't need to drown my sorrows, but I am not about to pass up free gin."

"Honey," Rainbow said, stowing the flask back in her locker, "it may just be time to hang up your silks."

"Bullshit." Bubbles stripped off the garments in question, and tossed them in a basket for cleaning. "Never happen."

"Listen to you, acting all tough," called Sunshine from the next bank of lockers. "Keep this up, you're gonna explode, I swear it."

"You never swear, Sunny. And I am not even going to dignify that with an answer," Bubbles said. She wrapped a rough towel around her, and marched off to the shower.

Maybe a cold shower would just wash away the frustration.

It wasn't that she didn't like Alphonse well enough. Hell, if she wasn't a jockey, she might even give him a tumble, but it would mean losing her job, her career, and for what?

As Bubbles dressed, Rainbow and Sunshine continued to taunt her. Finally, when all three were leaving the locker room, Rainbow threw a friendly arm over Bubbles' shoulder.

"You aren't the only one, you know," she whispered confidentially. "We've all thought about it."

"No shit. Like that's a big surprise."

"No, really," Sunshine said, earnestly. "We do think about it. How can you not?"

"But there's nothing we can do about it. Not if we want to keep our jobs. One little tumble, and poof!" Bubbles waved her hands. "Remember Tatiana? She had some scheme that was supposed to fool *Angel Heart*."

Sunshine's big blue eyes grew wide, and a single, perfect tear formed in one corner. "That poor girl! She was in the hospital for months when he threw her!"

Bubbles snorted in disgust. "Well, duh! Thought she could fool a unicorn? Hello! Magical creatures here, not gonna be fooled by some bimbo with a hormone overload."

Rainbow patted Bubbles on the back, as the three women made their way into the now-deserted parking lot. "You try to act like you're all hard-hearted and don't care, but we know better, Bubby. And we know Alphonse is pretty sweet on you, too."

Sunshine's mouth turned down at the corners, and she cocked her head to the side. "It's all sad and tragic, you know. Throwing away all that for a job."

"It's not all that, it's just a little roll in hay. Literally, if Tatiana is any example. And it's way more than a job, anyway," Bubbles shot back. "It's like my entire life. Racing is everything."

Rainbow's ancient Honda, painted in rainbow colors, and covered with decals from all the tracks they had visited, sat in the far corner of the lot.

The three women piled in, and Rainbow headed for The Finish Line, the local track hangout.

At a table in the jockey's corner, they had a beer, and the conversation picked up where it had left off.

They were nearly shouting over the din in the bar, the blaring jukebox providing a base for the buzz of conversation, punctuated by occasional shrill, alcohol-fueled laughter.

"I say go for it." Rainbow was not going to let it drop.

Bubbles shook her head. "Do I look like I am insane? Even if I am hot for his frame – which I am not, thank you very much – but even if I was, what am I gonna do? Throw away my entire life?"

"For love?" Sunshine asked, dreamily. "I can't think of a better reason." She sighed, a drawn-out, dramatic exhalation. "It must be wonderful to have someone love you."

"Sunny, get a grip! I don't love Al." Bubbles turned to glare at Rainbow. "And I am not hot for him, either."

Rainbow raised a skeptical eyebrow, but she didn't argue.

Across the bar, Alphonse watched Bubbles. She hadn't seen him when she came in, and he knew better than to approach a jockey in The Finish Line. The women jockey's corner was strictly off-limits to men.

She was a lost cause. Every time he got close to her, she turned as prickly as a cactus, all sharp points and attitude to spare.

That was the thing about the jockeys. They might be virgins, but they weren't all sweetness-and-light, oh no, not by a long shot. Most of 'em were kind of nasty when you got right down to it.

So why was he still watching Bubbles sip her beer?

Maybe <u>he</u> was the lost cause.

———

B ubbles paced the floor of her apartment. It was late, but she had a beer buzz, and she didn't want to sleep.

She stomped through the tiny area she laughingly called a living room, sidestepping her broken-down recliner, and dodging a basket of unfolded laundry.

She tried not to think about Al, about how it felt when she kissed him. Well, duh! She might be a rider – a virgin – but it didn't' mean she was dead or something. Everything worked just fine, thank you.

She glanced at the kitchen, a wall of counters with a miniature refrigerator, a two-burner cook top, and a single sink piled with dirty dishes. Not that she needed anything more elaborate. Had to stay at her racing weight, after all.

She yanked open the refrigerator door, wondering if, by some miracle, she had a beer hidden in there, and glared at the contents. Some wilted salad, a take-out container from Wong Lee's – steamed rice and broccoli – that she couldn't remember ordering. No beer.

Probably a good thing. It would mean an extra hour in the gym, sweating off the calories that came with the cold, golden goodness that came in that can. Even a light beer – yuck! – would cost her.

She slammed the refrigerator door, the thought of a beer reminding her of the conversation in the Finish Line. Her parts worked just fine, she just chose not to use some of them. It was a personal decision. Someday she might change her mind, but for now, some things were just more important than sex.

Oh, Sunshine would insist Bubbles was in love with Al, which was so totally not true. And Rainbow would tell her everybody had to hang it up sometime, that nobody raced forever, and there were other things she could do.

What did they know?

She growled, wishing they were here so she could tell them how wrong they were. She was so not ready to quit racing. She loved the excitement of the race, the feeling that she got when she rode a winner. She even enjoyed the feeling of being in Alphonse's arms, and the tinglies that came from kissing him.

But kissing would lead to more, and more would lead to even <u>more,</u> and before she knew it, she could be out of racing, and thinking about a second career.

No. Better she didn't even start down that road.

She paced back through the living room, slammed her fist against a lumpy cushion that sat in the recliner, and stomped into the bathroom. She needed another cold shower.

I n the changing room, the jockeys were in the usual state of pre-race jitters. Rainbow was standing in front of her locker, fingering her assortment of lucky charms, including the four-leaf clover she had found on a recent picnic.

Rainbow hadn't said much about it, but Bubbles knew it involved a man, and the clover had become a talisman for Rainbow. Judging by the goofy smile on her face, <u>there</u> was a girl who was getting ready to hang up her silks.

Not Bubbles.

Bubbles' talisman, if you could call it that, was a battered jockey's cap she had picked up after <u>Angel Heart</u> had thrown Tatiana. Every time she looked at it, she was reminded of Tatiana, who had tried to have it all.

And look where that got her. She slammed the door on the cap, her resolve stiffening her spine.

"Take it easy."

Bubbles looked up to find Sunshine looking at her pityingly, her big blue eyes round and solemn.

"What is your problem?" Bubbles growled.

Sunshine just shook her head. Rainbow turned, her face an angry red. "Could you both just keep it down? Some of us have to work today! Just because your boyfriend gives you the best runners, Bubby, doesn't give you the right to screw with the rest of us."

Bubbles sighed with disgust. "He is not my boyfriend. And I get the rides I deserve." She waved a hand in dismissal. "Whatever. Just get over your attitude before you get out on the track."

Bubbles turned her back on Rainbow, and caught Sunshine's wide eyes. She hooked a thumb over her shoulder, in Rainbow's direction. "I think we know who's horny today," she muttered.

"Take that back!"

Rainbow was on her in a flash, all elbows and bony fingers, digging into Bubbles unpadded ribs.

Bubbles went down, with Rainbow astride her, pinning her to the cold concrete floor of the changing room.

"Take it back!"

Bubbles bit her lip and refused to speak. Rainbow was constantly on her ass about Al. It was about time she had a dose of her own medicine.

"I swear, Bubbles, I don't have to take this -- "

Rainbow was jerked backwards, her words cut off, her face shocked.

Behind her, Bubbles could see Sunshine, tears streaming down her face. "Stop it!" she screamed. "Both of you, just stop it! I can't stand it when you fight."

Bubbles climbed slowly to her feet, brushing off her silks. Though the floor was clean, the gesture gave her a minute to collect herself.

She gave Rainbow a hard look, then turned her attention to Sunny. She had stopped crying, but her nose was red and swollen, and her eyes were puffy.

Bubbles felt instantly contrite for upsetting Sunny, even if Rainbow <u>was</u> acting like a jerk. "Sorry, Sunny. But you have to admit, she was being a bitch."

Rainbow was back on her feet, the color high in her cheeks, and her breathing fast. She took a step toward Bubbles, lifting her fists in front of her, then shook her head and backed away.

"Aw, hell!" she said, slapping her locker shut. The clang of metal-on-metal echoed off the bare walls of the room. "You may be right." She turned around to face Bubbles. "But it takes one to know one."

Rainbow stamped away, the sound of her boots clicking against the concrete fading as she disappeared through the door to the paddock.

Sunshine stared after her, her face troubled. "Oh, Bubby," she wailed. "I don't think I've ever seen her that way."

Bubbles sat down on the hard bench in front of her locker. "Neither have I, Sunny. Ever."

Bubbles winced as a thought struck her. "I don't act like that, do I? I mean, you guys are on me all the time, and I was just dishing it back. But I'm not like that."

"Well," Sunshine dropped down onto the bench beside Bubbles, and slipped her arm around her friend's narrow shoulders. "You do get a little crabby now and then. Especially when you've been around Al. Not that it's all that bad," she added hastily, as Bubbles tensed. "Not really that bad at all. Just sometimes ..."

Her voice trailed off, and she drew back. "No, not that

bad." She stood quickly, her voice suddenly brisk and unemotional. "I better go make sure Rainbow's okay."

———————

The last race of the day was a big one, and Bubbles was up on *Fairy Dust* again. The two of them seemed to understand each other, and riding him was usually a pure joy.

But today wasn't one of those days. As they broke from the gate, he surged into the lead, refusing her attempts to slow him down, to set the pace for their run.

Again and again, *Fairy Dust* fought her control. He would not hold back, wouldn't let the other runners tire themselves out. Instead, he forced himself faster and faster with each length.

Bubbles could feel him beginning to tire. His stride wasn't as sure, and when another unicorn pulled up on the inside, he hesitated before trying to cut him off.

Bubbles felt a surge of disappointment, then anger, as *Foo Foo Fifi* went by on her left, Sunshine hunched over his neck, urging him on.

She raised her whip, a tactic she almost never used on *Fairy Dust*, pushed herself forward, flattening her body against the big animal's neck.

"Run, you son-of-a-bitch!" she shouted, tapping him lightly on the flank with her whip. She didn't need to hit him, never had needed the whip, and she wasn't about to start now.

But she wasn't about to lose, either.

She felt *Fairy Dust* falter again, then he regained his footing, and his stride steadied.

Then began to pull ahead of the pack, leaving the rest of the racers behind. All except Sunshine and <u>Fifi</u>.

They rounded the last turn, the two racers so close that the announcer had fallen momentarily silent. There was no way to say who was in the lead.

The finish line was in straight ahead, and neither unicorn was giving an inch.

In the last five lengths, with the rest of the field bearing down on them, <u>Fifi</u> stumbled. He brushed against *Fairy Dust*, and for one sickening moment, Bubbles thought they were going down.

Instead, Sunshine pulled up on her mount, taking him closer to the rail, and out of the path of Bubbles and *Fairy Dust*.

It was over in an instant. *Fairy Dust* flashed across finish line, with <u>Fifi</u> a length behind.

Relief flowed through Bubbles. She had won, despite her ride's erratic behavior. This was what it was all about.

Bubbles let the reins lay slack against the unicorn's neck. She stood easily in the stirrups, leaning forward to pat her facing partner. They were a good team, even if he was acting peculiar today.

Then *Fairy Dust* reared, his front feet pawing the air. He snorted once, and twisted beneath her.

Bubble's stomach dropped with a sickening wrench, as her feet left the stirrups, and she went flying through the air.

She landed on her back, on the hard-packed dirt of the track, her breath knocked from her lungs, and one leg twisted beneath her.

For one long, agonizing moment, she was afraid to move. Broken bones were a fact of the racing life, and she'd had her share. Still, they weren't her idea of a good time.

She stirred, but before she could sit up, the medics were at her side, forcing her back down. They poked and prodded for long minutes, before they would let her up.

She struggled into a sitting position on the hard ground. Waiting behind the medics were her crew: Sunshine, tears welling in her eyes – that girl cried for anything! – and Rainbow.

And beside them was Al. Dear, sweet Al. Who had put her up on a mount that damn near killed her.

"What the hell is his problem?" she stormed at Al.

His eyes widened, and he took a small step back, but then he seemed sort of mentally shake himself, and he moved up close to her.

"His problem? Nothing much. Except that filly that was in the barn earlier today. Got him all riled up."

Al ran his eyes over her. Her silks were dusty and twisted around from the medic's inspection. Her helmet was askew, hanging over one ear and uncovering a serious case of helmet hair. Her face was covered with a light coat of dust, and there was a bruise already developing on one pale cheek.

She was beautiful.

"And I know exactly how he feels."

Al held out his hand, and she let him pull her to her feet. Nothing like a little brush with mortality to make a girl realize what was really important.

Al's arms went around her, and she lifted up on tiptoe. His lips found hers, and all those perfectly-working parts began to hum. The tinglies she had felt before intensified.

Just before she stopped thinking altogether, Bubbles made her choice.

What the hell. There were always other jobs.

A l watched from the rail, as his wife – his wife! – prepared for the between-races entertainment. We was proud of her, proud that she had found something she could excel at, even if it wasn't unicorn racing.

At least she was still working at the track.

In the infield, Bubbles adjusted the harness, and settled herself in the saddle. She waved at Al, a little shiver of pleasure passing through her, as she recalled the previous night. And anticipated the night to come.

This wasn't exactly unicorn racing, but it was still a respectable job.

She smiled at Al. He had been right, and so had Rainbow and Sunshine, who stood with him at the rail.

She braced herself, as the cow's muscles bunched beneath her. The cat raised his fiddle, and Bubbles took a deep breath.

"To the moon!" she whispered.

ALL ABOUT THE BALL

RAY VUKCEVICH

Ray Vukcevich has been publishing stories for decades in many of the top magazines. And back in the first incarnation of this magazine, I was lucky to get some of Ray's wonderful and very twisted short stories.

I am trying to put as many of his stories in these pages as I can because they always seem to be Pulphouse in style. And in voice.

That's right, Ray's voice is just amazing. Read the first paragraph of this story and you will understand why Ray fits in Pulphouse. You can find more of his stunning work at https://www.rayvuk.com/

ALL ABOUT THE BALL

RAY VUKCEVICH

INTERROGATION

Anyone looking down into that cold little room from the ceiling camera, say, will see two people sitting across from one another in folding chairs at a metal table bolted to the floor—the Meat and the Police Officer, but things are not quite that simple. The Meat is seven people, and the cop is at least two (the good cop and the bad cop), and one of the people in the Meat is dead. Her murder is the focus of the interchange between the still-living people in the Meat and the two cops.

I am one of the people in the Meat. My name is Nick. The Meat, that is to say the original personality, is actually called Mikhail Vodovos. Mikhail is in deep trouble over Yolanda's sudden death, and he knows it.

I see the entire scene in black and white, but that's just me. There are probably splashes of color. The cops might be wearing a red power tie. Those fuzzy spots swimming around the corners of Mikhail's vision might be blue or green or yellow. I couldn't tell you.

The walls of the interrogation room look flat white, but a lot of the paint has chipped off, revealing gray bricks underneath. The metal table is a darker gray than the walls under the paint and gleams dully in spots. The light comes from faintly humming florescent tubes, and the shadows all have sharp edges. Every detail has been carefully chosen, of course.

The police officer conducting the interrogation had introduced himself as Sergeant Billings and Sergeant Dumont. B and D, I'd thought. Dumont is probably female. It isn't hard to keep them straight, because they're doing the classic Good Cop/Bad Cop routine. They know we know they're doing it, and they seem to be just going through the motions with it. I am not fooled. I know a thing or two about interrogation techniques, and these two are obviously sharper than they want us to believe. They have a lot going on under the surface. For example, there is the rubber ball they hold in their right hand. It's about as big as a tomato, and I'm betting it's red.

Sergeant Billings, the good cop, looks at the ball in their hand, and then he looks at us, and then he looks back at the ball.

"It's like this, Mike," he says. "Do you mind if I call you Mike?" He doesn't wait for a reply. "We generally leave such family affairs alone. Someone kills someone in some head, and the dead person respawns, and the two of them kiss and make up. If no one files a complaint, it's nobody's business but their own. You follow me? But this is different, Mike..." Sergeant Billings continues, again stepping on any reply Mikhail might have made. I recognize what's going on: it isn't time for Mikhail to speak yet. It's time for Mikhail to realize that the jig is up, that they have the goods on him, that it is only a matter of time, and so on.

"…You went way too far this time. Not only did you give her neck a few sharp twists, but then you erased all of her backups. There will be no respawning for Yolanda. That last bit is the important part. That's where we have our problem. That's the part that makes this a serious crime, makes it murder, in fact. That's what makes it our business. Am I making all of this clear to you, Mike?"

But it's still not quite time for Mikhail to talk. "We have the 911 holograph recording, of course." Sergeant Billings pauses to let that sink in. "In this recording, we see the person you call 'the Animal' standing over the body. We want the Animal to come out and answer a few questions."

He holds the ball up about a foot or so above the table. I can feel Mikhail's heart pounding like crazy and smell his sweat. When Billings is sure everyone inside the Meat has gotten a good look, he drops the ball and then catches it as it bounces back up toward his hand. He does that again, and then a third time. And then he does it again. I know what he's up to. Obviously, he knows about the Animal and the Ball. He's trying to trick Archie (who the others call "The Animal," among other things that are similarly unkind) into coming out into the open. The fact that he knows about Archie's obsession with the Ball probably means he knows everything there is to know about all of us. They would have had crawlers all over the Clouds gathering information on us before they picked Mikhail up. They'd done their homework. That doesn't surprise me. Anyone can know everything about anything at any time, and the police even more so.

I can feel Archie tensing and crouching and focusing on the

Ball. For Archie, the Ball is not some childish game. The Ball is serious adult business. The Ball must be thrown. The Ball must be chased and caught and returned. The Cycle must be repeated. The welfare of the entire Multiverse depends on the Cycle.

Archie is in my lap, so I put a hand over his eyes. He could shift his sight around my fingers easily, but my gesture is enough to bring him back from the brink. Relief washes through the Meat. Mikhail must have let some of it show, because the cops close their hand on the bouncing ball and do their face changing routine again.

The bad cop says in her sharp tones, "I think you are all in it together."

Does that make any sense? Didn't the other cop just say that one of us had reported Yolanda's death? Who did that? I consider each of us one at a time starting with Mikhail (who no one calls "Mike"), the original personality that had developed "naturally" in the Meat, if it could be called natural—it seems pretty strange to me. Next had come Yolanda, who Mikhail had made to study physics which he had been interested in at the time. Apparently not interested enough to go out and study the subject himself, but interested enough to make an avatar to do it for him. It didn't take Yolanda long to "wake up" as the popular press puts it and demand she be allowed to branch off into cosmology. Mikhail had no choice but to let her do what she wanted, so he made Ricky, a first person shooter soldier dude, and turned him loose in an advanced War world where he happily slaughtered everything that moved.

Gabriela Fontane was next. The Butterfly Girl. She was supposed to be beautiful and smart and just all around fabulous, and she was, but she also was prone to dark periods of depression that not even new shoes could diminish. Mikhail thought a pet might help Gabby, so he made the Animal. The Animal started out as a "Tiny" in one of the classic Second Life Worlds, a Dachshund with huge black eyes and floppy ears who walked around on two legs like a very short human but considerably cuter. I don't think Mikhail expected the Animal to become a person, but it did. And when it did, it disappeared into a jungle world for nearly two years and didn't participate in Mergings with the rest of us at all. It turned out the Animal had spent months pouring over databases of scanned animal brains, adding who knew what.

I came next, Nick, the PI, and his black and white world. I hated being a private investigator and threw away my stupid fedora and dropped that nonsense as soon as I had any say in the matter. I worked for a while as a small town cop before drifting off into drink and existential angst. I might still be doing that, but the Animal suddenly returned and became my dog, you might say. I named him Archie, and he didn't seem to mind. Since he had become a person, he couldn't actually be my dog. He was more like my inscrutable friend. When he finally joined the Merging, he brought images of the hunt, the chase, the kill, the blood, the eating. It was pretty good. I think he liked me because I was the only one of us who would throw the Ball more than once or twice. In fact, I would throw it almost (but not quite) as long as he wanted to chase it.

After me there was Aaron, who Mikhail made to go off on trips around the world and bring us his experiences. Aaron was just back from Brazil when Yolanda was killed.

"Since you are all implicated in the murder," the bad cop

says, "there won't be any trickiness involved when you all go down for the crime."

I look over at the mirror and see the officer and Mikhail. Probably a two-way mirror. Who knows who is out there watching? Mikhail glances around like a cornered animal. He licks his lips. He opens his mouth and then he shakes his head and closes his mouth.

Stop that, I tell him. *You're just telegraphing that what she's saying is one hundred percent correct.* Someone else should be talking to the cops, but I need to keep Archie calm and out of the picture, so it can't be me. *Gabby, get out there and talk to them.*

Me? Why me? She says that in a way that makes me realize that she's the one who called 911 in the first place.

You know why, I say.

She doesn't have anything to say to that, which confirms my guess. Does that mean I can cross her off my suspects list? Absolutely not. Calling for help might just be part of her plan.

Gabby comes up to the front. "That's ridiculous, Sargent Dumont," she says. Using the bad cop's name is a nice touch. It lets them know we are having no trouble telling them apart. It tells them we have some confidence. That alone goes a long way toward canceling out Mikhail's sweating and fidgeting. "Why would we call the authorities if we had some kind of conspiracy going on?"

"Miss Fontane," the good cop says. "Shall we go over what you reported to the 911 system and get a few things cleared up?"

The bad cop comes back before Gabby can reply. "Even if you are not all in on it, at least one of you is. There is no way someone from outside Mikhail Vodovos could have killed

Yolanda Kane. We know the Animal is involved. We just don't know if it was acting alone."

They change their facial expression again, and the good cop says, "Here's what happened..." He manifests the 911 holographic recording of Gabby's call for help, and there it all is. They are in the Library. Yolanda is on the floor, sprawled on her stomach but with her head turned all the way around to face up at the ceiling. Archie is standing over her. It's easy to think of him as the Animal in this picture. He is a classic Manticore with the dull red body of a lion and a human head — vaguely human anyway. The head is too big, the eyes too round and too flat, the gaping mouth with too many rows of sharp teeth. He has wings like a bat, but it doesn't look like he could actually fly. He has the tail of a scorpion.

But wait a minute. If Yolanda is dead, what's maintaining her shape there on the floor? Maybe she'll just get up and twist her head around straight and give the Animal (she calls him Sparky because that seems to irritate him) a good swift kick. But no, here is a tablecloth moving across the room like a magic carpet. When it's positioned itself directly over Yolanda, it goes limp and drifts down and covers her. I can still see her shape under there. Someone screams.

I see it's Gabby, standing by the Library door, her big butterfly wings spread wide. This must be Gabby's re-creation. This couldn't have been recorded live as she called 911. This must be part of the mental dump she provided in the heat of the emergency.

"You!" she yells in the recording.

The Animal looks up at her. It crouches as though to leap across the room, but then ducks its head under the tablecloth covering Yolanda. There is a horrible slurping sound. The

Animal pulls its head back out and spins away and is gone in an instant.

Things don't look so good for Archie.

"So, it seems pretty clear," Sergeant Billings says. "The Animal killed Yolanda. Miss Fontane came upon the crime scene and called it in. Now we need to talk to the Animal. None of you is going anywhere until that happens."

Gabby, I say, *ask him how he knows Yolanda is dead. If the body is still there under that tablecloth…*

"What?" Gabby asks, speaking out loud.

"What, what?" the cop asks.

Maybe Yolanda is not even dead, I say. *Maybe we can still make this all come out okay.*

Archie whimpers in my lap, and I scratch him between the ears. After we'd been arrested, he'd returned in his Dachshund form, short gray coat (reddish brown to everyone else) and black eyes like glass. He's pretty cute when he's like this. He knows this is my favorite of his looks. He always uses it when he wants to be comforted or when he wants to work with the Ball.

It'll be okay, I mutter.

Are you crazy? Gabby sounds astonished. She inserts herself into our local rendering of the holographic presentation in the head and marches over to Yolanda's body. She bends and grabs the tablecloth and jerks it away like that magic trick where everything stays in place on the dinner table when the cloth is snatched from underneath.

There is nothing under the tablecloth.

Sergeant Billings says, "Subsequent research shows all traces of Yolanda in the Clouds disappeared the moment the Animal did whatever it did under that cloth. Some glimmer of her undoubtedly exists in your Meat, but even if she were rebuilt, she would never be the same—that's what makes this a clear murder. Now send out the Animal."

We need to stall a little longer while I figure this out, I tell the others. *We're overlooking something.*

Like you're going to figure it out, Gabby says.

I am the detective, I say.

She laughs.

I simply can't believe Archie killed Yolanda. Mikhail has to be the main suspect. Or Gabby. They are the ones most upset by the worldview Yolanda introduced into the Meat, the worldview that cannot be true, but probably is.

JUST THE FACTS

Yolanda's post doc work in Cosmology had focused on Special Relativity and the Relativity of Simultaneity, where two observers moving relative to one another will disagree on which events are happening Now. Events considered to be in the past or the future (depending on how they are moving in relation to one another) of one might be in the present of the other. Past, present, and future events are all equally real in space-time. Which means you can no more change the future than you can change the past. There is no such thing as classic free will.

Yolanda also told us how multiple universes arise in almost every theory of physics. Everything that can happen does happen somewhere in the Multiverse. So, she explained, the purpose of life is finding out which universe you happen to be in and seeing how it all plays out. It's like you are a character in a book that no one wrote. You have no idea what's in the upcoming pages, and you can't change anything that you will do, but that doesn't mean you don't have to make choices.

Mikhail and Gabby did not accept any of this even if they couldn't come up with any arguments against it. Ricky didn't give a rat's ass, and Aaron had places to go and people to see.

I am not just a character in some book! Gabby would shout.

Well, Mikhail did make you, Yolanda would say.

And who made me? Mikhail would ask.

We all make ourselves! Gabby would shout.

And so on.

MALICE AFORETHOUGHT

So, there had been some friction in that area, but would Gabby or Mikhail kill Yolanda over philosophy? Well, I suppose people have committed murder for stranger reasons. I can easily imagine Gabby setting Yolanda on fire or pushing her off a building, but someone had coldly and with malice afore-thought erased Yolanda. This was not a sudden crime of passion. More like Mikhail than Gabby.

We should switch again, I say. *Buy us some more time. Someone else get out there and talk, and you come back inside, Gabby.*

I'll go, Ricky, our action figure, says.

Good, I say. *But no shooting.*

I am only half joking, and he knows it. Things could go from bad to horrible if Ricky decides this is a situation that demands no subtlety.

Once Ricky starts talking, I tune him out to think about motives and opportunities. Ricky's chatter is irrelevant. It will have to do with caliber or fire rate, and Ricky will be saying that if he had killed Yolanda he would have used a shotgun or maybe a grenade. And the cops, one or the other of them, will be telling him to shut the fuck up and send out the Animal.

Maybe Ricky did do it. Why else had he volunteered to go out and talk to the cops? This is not an action sequence. He has no expertise in this area. If anyone should be talking to the cops, it should be Aaron, the world traveler who is all the time interacting with strange people in strange places. Why hadn't he volunteered? Had Aaron come home and killed Yolanda?

"Well, it's like this, officer," Ricky says.

There is a commotion, and Ricky doesn't finish his thought.

"What the hell just happened?" one of the cops asks.

Gabby screams again.

I poke around in the Meat, expand myself into all of our brain rooms, but Ricky is gone. Not gone like he'd walked on down to the corner for a beer, but gone in the same sense Yolanda is now gone.

Two things. First, I can take Ricky off the suspects list, and second, but more important, whoever killed Yolanda and Ricky must be trying to kill us all! Who's next? And who's doing this? Aaron, Gabby, or Mikhail himself?

Out in the so-called Real World, Mikhail had been jerked to the forefront when Ricky disappeared, and he had slumped forward onto the table. The cops had leaped up and called out or jabbed buttons or something because there are suddenly a lot of people and even more confusion pushing into the little interrogation room.

Mikhail's sudden seizure doesn't fool me.

Mikhail, I say quietly. *Why don't we just Merge now and see who the killer is?*

I don't think that's a good idea at this point, Nick. Mikhail sounds calm and cold and not at all like a guy who has just passed out on a table. He had simply come back inside and let the Meat go limp.

It's you, isn't it? I ask him. It makes sense. Who else would want to kill us all off? Mikhail must want to start over with new people. He doesn't love us anymore.

Don't be ridiculous, Nick, he says. *What kind of detective are you anyway?*

No kind of detective, I might have told him. I never asked for this black and white bullshit. If I live through this, I'm going to take my dog and head out to the woods for a few years and get in touch with nature or whatever.

They've flopped the Meat onto his back on the table and someone is peeling back his eyelids and listening to his heart and slapping his wrists and his cheeks.

Back in our head, Aaron runs into the Library. He's naked except for a cheap white bathrobe hanging open with the logo of a major hotel chain above the little pocket in the front.

You think Mikhail is trying to kill us? he asks.

Well, maybe, I think, but it just as well might be you. But it isn't. Aaron explodes, sending bloody body parts shooting out in all directions. I slow everything down and step into the stacks just in time to miss being splattered. In the Nick of Time. Ha ha. Aaron dead, too? I feel the hard rubber edge of the oxygen mask as it is clamped down over Mikhail's face.

Nick? Gabby flutters near the high ceiling on unfurled wings. *What's happening to us, Nick? Is it really Mikhail? You wouldn't hurt me, would you, Mikhail? Nick?*

Then she goes up in a pssft of flames from bottom to top with nothing but a little squeak and falling ashes like a paper with the secret code on it that you burn in an emergency so the bad guys can't read it.

This is it. Mikhail killed them all except for me and my little dog. We have to be next. Out in the Real World, it will probably be judged some kind of brain seizure. Maybe Mikhail will get some medical rehabilitation, learn to walk and talk again, so sad, and later when all of this is behind him, he'll cautiously make some new people. Of course he'll make them. He will be encouraged to make new people. You just can't be fully human these days without the transcendental experience of the Merging. Making new people will be part of his therapy. It will take time, but he'll have good doctors and lots of support. Someone will write up his case, and students will study it for years to come.

Surely, he can't get away with it. Surely, this is not the first time the original person in the Meat has wanted to get rid of the newcomers who have not worked out as expected. Surely, the cops will see right through all of this when Mikhail is the last man standing.

You'll never get away with it, Mikhail, I say.

What? He sounds frightened. *Nick? Don't. Wait. Stop...*

Blood fills the head. Blood everywhere. Much worse than when Aaron went. It washes through the head's hallways and floods the Library. Books float away on rivers of blood. There's a terrific wind and the sound of millions of leaf blowers and chainsaws. There is a tremendous bang, and then all goes still. Things are subtly different. The details are not so bright.

What is this? I ask. *Mikhail? Mikhail!*

"This doesn't look good," someone out in the Real World says. The frenzied activity out there has subsided. Only the two cops in one and a guy who has to be a doctor are left.

Things are pretty quiet inside, too. I feel around for Mikhail, but I don't find him. There are holes where Yolanda and Ricky and Aaron and Gabby and Mikhail used to be. There are faint echoes of them all. Or maybe that is my imagination.

So where does all this leave me?

I look down into the gleaming black eyes of the little dog in my lap.

THE BALL

This might be Central Park judging by the skyline beyond the greenery, but we don't think it is. At least it isn't Real Life Manhattan which has no zeppelins swimming between the buildings. Nick is sitting on a bench with a restless little dog in his lap.

Nick puts Archie down on the ground. Archie twists around and runs a short distance and then turns back and barks twice at Nick.

The Ball! The Ball!

Nick has no ball. "Sorry," he says, and shows the dog his empty hands.

Archie paws at the ground. He curls his lips back over his teeth and snarls a low deep sound then yaps again.

Things have fallen completely apart. The others are dead, the worlds they'd lived in drifting away. Yes, there are traces of them all, but they would never be the same people they had been even if they could be rebuilt, and Nick has no idea how to do that anyway.

That leaves the Animal and the Ball and the Person Who Throws the Ball. The Animal has taken over, and any new person introduced will have something to do with the Ball.

Nick had been too busy trying to be the detective he never

was, ignoring the obvious and trying to dig deeper. It had been bad enough to be a black and white detective, but now he was going to be the guy who endlessly threw a ball for a little dog.

"I don't think so," Nick says.

Archie expands in all directions like he is being blown up from the inside, and he has only to take a single step to be right up in Nick's face. The Animal is the Manticore again and then he is the Griffin. He is the Lion, he is the Bear, he is the Tiger, and then he is the Big Bad Wolf. His jaws are big and horrible and the mouth wide, and the teeth razor sharp, and there are rows and rows of them, and the jaws come down over Nick and bite him in half at the waist. The Animal swallows the top half of him and then gulps down the bottom half.

We realize that this is what the Merging will be like from now on. No more happy transcendental orgies. The Animal will send his parts into the worlds, and at the end of the day he will eat them, and we will be what we were always meant to be. The Ball is not a game. The Ball is serious business. The Ball is like a poem describing everything. A poem needs words like this thing needs a Ball to throw and a Ball to chase and a Ball to catch and a Ball to return. It is not that the process must be done over and over, but more that it is just one timeless process, one thing stretched over space-time and holding us together making us what we are which is an offshoot of the next stage in human evolution.

We want to surrender now. We want to sigh and relax and say to hell with it all, but one more thought that is not strictly speaking *our* thought, but is instead a thought unique to Nick, comes into our mind. He opens our eyes, jerks our arms up, and snatches the red rubber ball from the fist of the cops leaning over us, who are still holding it after everything that has gone on out there outside of us. Nick throws it hard across the cold little interrogation room, and it bounces off the mirror and zooms back at us, and the Animal leaps out after it.

The Animal cannot, of course, leap all the way out of our Meat here in the downtown police station, but he gets far enough out for Nick to slam the door on him. Once the door is closed, Nick expands into our brain and fills as much of it with himself as he can. The Animal struggles back in with the ball in his mouth, but it is too late.

"Sit," Nick says.

First appeared in the big click (online)

LOST FRIENDS
R.W. WALLACE

This original story is the second in a series of wonderful mystery stories from R. W. Wallace that have been in numbers of issues of Pulphouse.

But this story is not like any standard mystery. The detective is a ghost, limited to his own cemetery helping other ghosts move on by solving their problems. In other words, the detective is locked in a confined space with no tools, trying to help a victim discover what happened to them.

Great writing and some of the most innovative plotting I have seen in a long time. A wonderful series.

And for even more of her work, check out her website at http:// rwwallace.com/

LOST FRIENDS

R.W. WALLACE

A t the farthest corner of the cemetery, a very special mausoleum stands vigil. It's not particularly pretty, nor gaudy, nor pious. It's tall, solid, and spacious.

Some call it the pauper's grave, but that's not quite right either.

From what I've understood, the mausoleum was paid for according to the last wishes of a retired police detective, to give a final resting place to the Jane and John Does of the district, the bodies nobody claimed, nobody wanted.

The detective's urn is in there as well, in the spot directly across from the entrance, watching over all his charges.

At least, I imagine that was the idea. Except, as far as I know, the detective didn't linger after his burial, and the guarding has been left to us other ghosts.

Not that I mind.

Today, the mausoleum has a new arrival.

I stand leaning against Clothilde's tomb stone as we watch the party of three make their way from the church. Two police

181

officers and one priest. The youngest of the officers carries a simple, white urn against his chest, his fingers white from clutching it too hard.

He can't be more than twenty-five, probably fresh out of the academy. His hair is dark and curly despite being cut short, his eyes large and brown—and filled with unshed tears. While his colleague has a whispered discussion with the priest, the young man is clearly fighting demons in his own head as he focuses on their destination.

"Doesn't seem like we're getting a new friend," Clothilde comments. She's pretending to sit on her tomb stone. I say pretend because she's sitting at the right height, just not in the right location. Not wanting to get too close to me, she sits mid-air right next to the slab of black stone, hands beneath her thighs and swinging her legs.

Most of us try to respect the physical laws of the living even if we don't have to. Clothilde doesn't.

"Doesn't hurt to stay to watch," I reply. "A couple of extra witnesses."

When the small procession passes us, we stand to follow. I sidle up right behind the older officer and the priest, unapologetically eavesdropping.

"How old did you say she was?" the priest asks in a whisper.

"Nine or ten. Probably. Hard to tell when they're undernourished like that."

"You're certain she was murdered, didn't just die of hunger?"

The officer's torso swelled as it filled with anger. "I'd argue that a kid dying of hunger *is* a murder." He deflated a little.

"But yeah. Marks on her neck, skin under her nails, bruises all over. She was murdered."

"So you have DNA?"

"No match." A sigh. "If he ever pops up in our database later, we'll nail him, but right now we're stuck."

I share a look with Clothilde. Sounds like someone who'd have unfinished business, who'd want to stick around for a bit to tie up loose ends. But the silence from the urn says otherwise.

A coffin or urn will only let a ghost free once he or she has accepted they're dead. This usually means days of screaming and pounding.

A silent urn means the girl has already moved on.

"You have nothing?" the priest asks. His eyes glide over to the younger officer walking in front of him, compassion marking his features.

The older officer huffs. "Normally, I'd tell you I can't talk about an ongoing investigation, but there's really nothing to tell. All we have is a dead body and useless DNA."

"Where was she found?"

"At the bottom of a cliff in the forest outside of town. She was dead before she was thrown down there," he adds before the priest can ask. "It seems they considered that ravine like a convenient place to throw away a body." His voice lowered. "Was found by a couple of young boys going on an adventure."

We reach the mausoleum and the priest takes the urn. He slides it into the designated slot and closes the little door.

Like with most of the slots here, there is no name, only a cross and a date of death.

The priest says a few words, more than he usually does in

here—I'm guessing it's for the young officer's benefit, who seems on the verge of collapsing from keeping his tears back—then they turn to leave.

Clothilde and I stay back, on the front steps of the mausoleum, and watch them exit the cemetery. The priest goes back to the church, the two officers leave in an unmarked car.

"Who are you?" says a voice from behind us. "Where am I?"

I whirl around. If I'd had a beating heart, it might just have stopped beating.

In the middle of the mausoleum, dirty feet on the black-and-white checkered floor, stands a girl of nine or ten. Malnourished and so thin it's painful to watch, large clear eyes staring at me.

"Where are my friends?" she asks. "They were supposed to be here."

———

"Where are my friends?" the girl asks again when she gets no answer from us, her voice serious. Her arms hang limply at her side, almost swallowed in the several-sizes-too-big t-shirt she's wearing.

I finally find my voice. "I'm afraid your friends aren't here, honey."

She flashes her teeth in a snarl and hisses. "Don't call me honey."

I raise my hands in surrender. "Okay, I won't. I promise. Do you have a name, perhaps?"

Her distrust is clear as she considers whether or not to give me her name. Her gaze takes in the mausoleum, the cemetery outside, the gray-scale ghosts talking to her. "Rose," she says.

"That's a lovely name," I tell her. "It suits you."

"No, it doesn't," she spits. "Roses are beautiful and full of life. Roses are free."

Clothilde speaks in that midnight voice she sometimes uses when emotions are close to the surface. "Roses have thorns. They can make even the biggest man bleed."

Rose studies Clothilde. I wonder if she knows to recognize clothes that were at the height of fashion in the eighties. If she sees the anger that Clothilde carries like a blanket but will never share with anyone. If she sees the danger lurking.

Rose smiles. "I like you. What's your name?"

"Clothilde."

Rose nods, a mischievous smile making her go from street urchin to long-lost warrior princess. "Clothilde, you and I are going to be the best of friends."

Somehow, I don't think that means what I think it means.

Clothilde knows it, too. She takes her time considering the little girl in front of us, measuring her up against God knows what. She gives a tiny nod. "Done."

"Excellent." Rose claps her hands as if to get the party going. "Now, where are my friends?"

I've never had to do this before. Something must have gone wrong with the urn, because it's not supposed to let her out until she knows she's a ghost. This girl just walked out thinking she must have fallen asleep or something, and expects to find her friends.

I have to tell her she's dead.

"Your friends aren't here, Rose," I explain. "Something

happened to you, and now you're..." I wave a hand to the cemetery behind me. "You're dead."

I hold my breath, waiting for the denial or the panic. Or both.

Rose rolls her eyes at me. "I know I'm dead, stupid. You don't think I'd remember dying?"

I'm floored, unable to catch a breath I don't need, my brain not able to wrap itself around what she said.

"You know you're dead?" I ask. Maybe I heard her wrong.

Rose's eyes wander from my head to my toes, then comes back up. "You don't?"

I blink. Shake myself back into action. "Of course I know I'm dead. I've been here for over thirty years." I fall down on my knees so I'm not towering above the little girl. "How did *you* know?"

She shrugs and flashes an uncertain look at Clothilde. "It's what always happens when one of us is brought into the woods in the middle of the night. It was either me or Violette," she explains when she doesn't understand why I look so shocked. "We're the oldest."

"How many of you are there?" I whisper.

"Twelve," Rose answers. "But I think he has his eyes on a new one, so he had to make room for her."

"A new what?" I think I know the answer, but I have to ask.

"A new girl. He likes 'em young and smooth," she says. She's mimicking a coarse accent, what you'd expect from a guy living in the middle of nowhere. "Puberty is messy," she continues. "Doesn't want to deal with that."

Puberty? "How old are you?"

For the first time, she looks uncertain. She stares down at her bare feet. "I don't know. I was five when he got me."

"And how did he 'get you?'"

"Snatched me in the park. Drove for a long time. Put me in the house."

I sit back on my heels, mind reeling.

Clothilde takes over the questioning. "Why did you expect to meet your friends here, if you know you're a ghost?"

Rose wraps her arms around herself, as if she can feel the cold. "Everybody comes back when they're taken to the woods. They keep us company. Look after us."

Clothilde swears under her breath. "They come back as ghosts when they die?"

Rose nods.

"And you could see them?"

Rose pulls a face. "Not really see them. Feel them. They'll sit with us when we're punished, keep us company when it's our turn with the old man. Sing to us when we can't sleep."

"Old man?"

"It's what he wanted us to call him."

Clothilde paces back and forth inside the mausoleum, her feet a couple of inches above the floor. "If they stay in the house as ghosts," she says to me, "it means they're buried nearby."

"Probably," I say. I'm still on my knees in front of the little girl. I want to give her a hug, but don't think it's a good idea. "We don't have experience with anyone buried outside of the cemetery. We don't know how it works out there."

Clothilde points her thumb at Rose. "Why didn't he bury her with the rest of them?"

I shake my head as I ponder this new mystery.

"Did the old man ever get bothered by the ghosts?" I ask.

Rose nods. "When there are many ghosts together, we can feel them better. Some time ago, Petunia came back earlier than usual because the old man started freaking out. She said our friends helped her."

Clothilde stopped her pacing and cocked her head at Rose. "Why do you all have flower names?"

"It's the names he gives us when we arrive. If you try to tell anyone your real name, you get taken into the woods straight away."

Clothilde puts a hand on the girl's shoulder, her voice soft. "What's your real name, sweetheart?"

Rose flinches at the nickname, but doesn't say anything. I'm guessing we should stay away from any nickname that bastard of an old man could have used.

"You can tell us," I say. "He can't hurt you now you're already dead."

She chews on her lip and her breathing accelerates. "Lena," she finally whispers.

"That suits you even better than Rose," Clothilde says with a smile. "I'm very happy to be your friend, Lena."

Lena smiles, but it's wobbly. Her eyes fill with tears and she hugs her arms closer around herself. "I want my friends."

I force myself not to take the girl in my arms. I'm afraid she won't appreciate being held by a man right now.

Luckily, Clothilde has the same impulse and envelops the girl in her arms, making the thin body almost disappear in her adult one. "We'll help you, Lena." She pulls the little girl's head away from her breast so she can look her in the eye. "But I don't think that what you really need is to meet your friends."

Tears streak down Lena's cheeks as she starts to whine.

"What you need," Clothilde says forcefully enough to get through to the little girl, "is to make sure the old man is punished. And save your living friends."

As the words register, the whines subside. Hiccups start up and the tears keep falling, but Lena's eyes widen in wonder. "I can do that?"

"There are no guarantees," I say as I push myself into a standing position. There are days like this, where I feel the age of my body despite not having felt my body in over three decades. "But we'll do our best to help you."

———

"W e're going to need outside help," I tell Clothilde. We're sitting on the steps of Lena's mausoleum while the girl makes the tour of the cemetery. We told her she wouldn't be able to leave, but—like all of us—she has to see it for herself.

"We *always* need outside help," Clothilde replies. "It's just a question of giving a nudge to the right person. In this case, there's a good chance we won't have any visitors—unless that sniveling officer comes back."

I tap my fingers on my thigh. "You know, there's a good chance he will. If he was that torn up about the case, he's not going to let it go."

"You did." Her voice is soft and her eyes distant.

"Which is why I'm here, still." I sigh. "And I didn't bawl my eyes out like that guy—he'll be back. We have to figure out what to do when he does."

"What do we want from him, exactly?"

"We need to give him clues," I say. "They said they were without leads, but we have information we can give them. Like a name."

"Is that all?" Clothilde rolls her eyes and leans back on her hands. "You know as well as I do that we can give them nudges, or communicate really strong feelings. We can't spell out a name for them."

She's right, of course. The height of influence we have on the living world is swatting away a fly, or blowing dust across the floor...

"We *can* spell it out!" I jump up and run over to the little door that's hiding Lena's urn. In front of the door, there's a small ledge. Spotless, because everything was cleaned before a new urn arrived, but it doesn't need to stay that way.

"Clothilde." I wave her over. "You're much better at this than me. Can you blow in some dust from the path outside, do you think? Get some of it up here? Then we should be able to spell the name in the dust."

I can see that Clothilde's first reaction is to refuse. A part of her is stuck as the rebellious teenager, but it only comes out occasionally. Now she glances over to the cemetery's back gate, where Lena has climbed the gate and is giving it her all to fall down on the other side.

"I'll give it a try," she says. "But there's no way I'll manage to cover only that ledge," she warns me. "This whole place is going to be a mess."

I stretch my arms out, leaving her the floor. "Have at it."

———

S he wasn't kidding about the mess. By the time she's done, there's a thick layer of dust all across the floor. The ledge in front of the urn's door has such a thin layer it's barely visible.

"That ledge is really high up," Clothilde says as she levels the ledge with a murderous stare.

"No worries," I tell her. "You did a great job. This should do the trick."

I step up to the ledge and hold a finger above the dust. I focus everything I have on making my finger as solid as possible, and on the fine particles I'd like to behave as if I had a solid form.

I don't get it on the first try, nor the tenth, of course. But I persevere. If there's something we have an infinite supply of here, it's time. So I stay in front of that ledge, pushing my finger through the dust over and over, until lines appear.

It's well into the next day when I declare myself finished. Clothilde has come and gone, spending the most time with Lena. The girl didn't have trouble accepting she was a ghost, but she's unable to grasp being stuck here, and not with her dead friends in the forest.

Two days later, the young officer is back. This time, he's alone and he's not trying to put on a brave face.

He shuffles into the mausoleum, head down and a single tear running down his chin.

When he sees all the dust on the floor, he freezes. "What the—"

He spins around in a circle, taking in the mess Clothilde made. His mouth is hanging open, his eyes are bugging out, his breathing is shallow.

"Who would do this?" He stomps around in a circle, kicking up dust, repeating with increasing volume, "Who would do this?"

"Go check on the urn, buddy," I tell him.

People can't actually hear us, of course. But their subconscious must hear us on some level, because most people will take a nudge.

The officer takes his time about it, though. In fact, he makes such a mess of—well, our mess—that I worry he'll ruin my work. I keep telling him to approach the ledge, check on the urn. And *finally*, he calms down and does as I tell him.

He stalks up to the little door. "I'm going to find out who did this," he fumes. "I'm going to find out who killed you, and who did this to your grave. I—"

He cuts himself short as he sees the writing. "What?—"

His head snaps around so fast, I cringe in compassion. He takes in the mess, and I see the moment he realizes he might have ruined potential evidence. He didn't, of course, but there's no way for me to tell him that.

"It was all smooth when I came in," he says to himself. "There were no footsteps. I would have noticed if there were footsteps." He puts his nose an inch above the writing on the ledge. "Then how did they write this? Lena?"

He straightens and his eyes go to the door hiding the urn. "Was that your name, little one?"

"Yes, it was." Lena herself has come, Clothilde at her heels. "My name was Lena."

The officer nods. "Guess it's worth looking into."

He snaps a few pictures, but leaves only a minute or two later. He has a spring to his step that I'm happy to see.

Lena slinks back out, Clothilde in tow, to try every single spot along the cemetery wall, in search of her friends.

———

I t's at least ten days until we get new visitors to the mausoleum. Lena has accepted that she can't leave the cemetery grounds, but she's no less restless.

On a bright Sunday morning, a couple in their late thirties park their car in the church's parking lot, and walk slowly through the cemetery. A police car arrived with them, but the driver—our young officer from earlier if I'm not mistaken—doesn't get out.

The woman's none too steady on her feet and I suspect the man's only doing better because he has the task of taking care of his wife.

I wait for them at the mausoleum. Lena and Clothilde join me, silent and serious.

"Do you remember these people?" I ask Lena.

A frown mars her little forehead and her hands are balled into fists at her sides. "I don't... I can't... I... Mommy?"

She steps forward, just in time for her mother to step right through her.

"Sorry about that," Clothilde says before the girl can get too upset. "Follow them inside. See what they have to say."

We all follow. Lena stands right in front of her resting place the better to see her parents' faces, while Clothilde and myself keep a respectful distance.

"I can't believe you were alive all these years," the mother sobs. "I'm so sorry we weren't able to find you, darling." She places a hand on the little door, not realizing she's touching her daughter's ghost's face.

Lena has the expression of an innocent five-year-old, not the weathered and angry ten-or-so-old we've gotten used to. The love in her eyes as she looks at her mother is blinding.

"At least now you can rest," the mother whispers. "I can't believe that's the best we can do."

"It's not all we can do," the father says. His voice is no more steady than his wife's and his worry lines are too deep for someone his age. "We'll also help the police find whoever did this to her."

The anger comes back to Lena's features. "The old man," she tells them. "He was mean to us. Hurt me. Hurt my friends. I miss my friends, Mommy. They need me."

The mother shakes her head, as if to remove cobwebs.

"I think she hears you," I say. "Continue talking about the old man. Try remembering what it was like there, and in the forest. Anything to help them find your friends."

She does as I tell her. What follows is a harrowing account of all the horrors she saw in that house in the woods, and of her friends, alive kids and ghosts alike.

The mother breaks down into sobs, only her husband holding her up. She won't understand why she feels this way, but I'm guessing she's gotten the gist of her daughter's message.

"See the writing in the dust, like the officer mentioned?" the husband says once she starts to calm down. "Somebody knew who she was and wanted her to be reconnected with her family."

Wiping away tears, the mother stares at my masterpiece. "This was done by a friend," she says. "Whoever did this to her didn't want her to be identified." She lifts her gaze to meet her husband's, the same determination we've seen in Lena as she attempted escape shining through. "We have to find that friend."

"The forest." Clothilde has moved closer, so close her mouth is superposed with the woman's ear. "Try the forest. Where she was found."

"The forest." Lena adds her voice in. "Search the forest, Mommy. Help my friends."

The mother sways on her feet, leans a hand against the wall. "Wasn't she found in a forest? How well did they search that place?"

"I think they did a pretty thorough search," the husband replies.

"Well, they're going to be more thorough. That officer told us they suspect whoever did this was behind at least ten other kidnappings in our town. If they're looking for ten kids instead of just one, they can damned well search ten times as far. They have to go through that *whole* thing!"

The husband kisses his wife's temple. "It's a pretty big forest, honey."

"They're going to *search* that forest. Or I'll never let them rest."

The husband nods. "Then that's what they'll do."

"Thank you, Mommy," Lena whispers. She leans in to give her mother a hug—she even gets it right the first time and doesn't go straight through.

Once her parents have driven away, Lena joins me on the steps of her mausoleum. "Do you think they'll find them?"

"It's out of our hands now, little one," I tell her. "But I hope they do. I really hope they do."

———

They did find the house. The old man—I still don't know his real name, and don't care to know—had had enough of the ghosts haunting his house and decided to get rid of the bodies farther away from his house. He'd walked far enough with Lena's body for the search party not to have reached his home on their first trip through, but not far enough to resist the search party Lena's mother managed to set up with the parents of the ten other missing children.

The old man was arrested, and is expected to spend the rest of his life in jail.

The twelve girls—one who'd arrived just two days after Lena's death as her replacement, also named Rose—who still lived at the house, were sent straight to the hospital for a check-up, then reunited with their families.

The parents who hadn't found their children requested a detailed check of the grounds around the house.

We learned all of this from Lena's mother, who came to give us daily updates. She'd clearly caught onto the importance her daughter put in saving her friends, and made sure she knew they were now safe at home with their families. They'd have some tough times ahead, but they'd live.

She'd also promised a surprise for today, which had all of us, including Clothilde who never got excited about anything, checking the parking lot every two minutes, asking each other what we thought the surprise would be.

Finally, as the sun approaches the horizon, a van pulls into the parking lot, and Lena's parents exit. As they start pulling open the back doors, several other cars follow, each one containing a couple or a family.

Every couple goes to the van, gets something from the back, and walks solemnly toward the cemetery.

"They're urns," Lena whispers.

I nod.

As the first couple passes the gate to the cemetery, a ghost exits the urn and looks around. It's a girl.

"Iris!" Lena exclaims and runs to throw herself at the new arrival. "They brought Iris! And Lily!"

A second girl has jumped out of the next urn, held by a Chinese couple accompanied by a boy of about five.

They're all here. Ghost tears run freely as the girls are reunited, touching each other's faces, giving kisses, screaming so loud I'm glad I no longer have ear drums.

The families all make their way to the mausoleum. They wait outside, letting Lena's mother go in first.

"Come, Lena," I tell her. "Let's see what your mother has to say."

We all squeeze in, the girls hovering above us in the air, clearly used to not respecting physical laws.

"I brought your friends, honey," Lena's mother says to her daughter's slot. "We found the place that awful man used as a mass grave. Now, we could all have brought you home to our cemeteries, but we didn't want to separate you."

A couple of mothers nod their heads at this, making me realize Lena must not be the only one to have influenced her parents.

"So we've brought you all here. The police told us it was okay, that it was the least they could to to repay us for finding the man who murdered you.

"Now you can play together as much as you like." A tear falls down her face and lands on the dirty floor with a plop.

What follows is a procession of families deposing the urns of their daughters' ashes in the mausoleum. There's not a dry eye in sight, living or ghosts alike.

When the families finally leave, I'm left with a host of young girls.

Who are already becoming more transparent.

Lena looks down at herself, then asks, "Is this it? Do we not get to play?"

If there was ever a group of kids who deserved to play, it was this one.

"I'm sure you'll be allowed to play where you're going," I tell her. "Take a good hold of each other's hands and stay together, okay?"

I have no idea if there's any point in doing it, but the girls follow my instructions. They all fade out at the same time just as a peal of joyous laughter sounds across the cemetery.

Clothilde stares longingly at the spot where Lena stood moments earlier. "You did good, detective." Then she ambles across the grounds toward her own tomb stone.

I swallow and think back on all my cases, before and after my death. This goes a good way toward redemption, I think, but there's still a long way to go.

A long, long way.

IT'S A WONDERFUL DEATH

ROBERT JESCHONEK

Robert Jeschonek continues his streak of being in every issue of Pulphouse Fiction Magazine.

The moment I read the title of this story, I knew it had to be in Pulphouse. The holiday issue, of course. Anyone who can twist that old movie is a genius in my book.

Robert's stories have appeared in dozens of magazines and he has published dozens of novels as well. He has even worked for DC Comics and early in his career sold me a couple stories when I was editing for Star Trek at Pocket Books. He seems to be able to do it all. And to see all the amazing projects he has done, check out his website at https://www.robertjeschonek.com/

IT'S A WONDERFUL DEATH

ROBERT JESCHONEK

"Elias Dalton." The haggard figure of a man in a shabby black suit and tie stood at the foot of the bed, scowling as mist swirled around him. "I have come to guide you in a life-changing journey on this dark and dismal Christmas Eve."

The bed's occupant, a slender man with a shaggy black mane and beard, opened his eyes, looking confused. "Who *are* you?" His voice was slurred. "How'd you get *in* here?"

"My name is Bertram," said the man in the suit. "And I go where my mission takes me, Mr. Dalton." Dramatically, he wove his long-fingered, black-gloved hands through the air. "For I am a *demon* of *Christmas!* Hell's own yuletide *ambassador,* come to call!"

Dalton frowned. "What mission?"

"To make you see the *light!*" said Bertram, and then he howled with ghostly laughter.

"Vital signs as expected," said the middle-aged blonde woman in the dark control room next-door. "The drugs have kicked in, and Elias Dalton is officially *tripping balls.*"

"Meaning we can tell the son of a bitch what we want him to hear, and he'll believe it." The bearded, dark-skinned man standing behind her, whose name was Newton Baker, nodded. "I just hope ol' Bertram can deliver."

"You know he can. We all can." The woman's green eyes behind gold wire-framed glasses were glued to a laptop screen on the folding table in front of her, watching Bertram and Dalton interact.

"More fog, please." Newton folded his arms over his chest. Like Mia, he was dressed all in black—black sweater, black jeans. "And pipe in more sulfur smell. We need to keep building the illusion that an actual demon's come to visit."

Mia turned knobs on a custom control board to the left of the laptop, adding to the swirling fog and sulfurous stench in the bedroom set. "Seriously, Bertram's a pro. He's on top of his game tonight."

"He wasn't last time." Newton snorted. "And the stakes weren't anywhere near *this* personal."

"He'll come through. I have faith in him." The woman, Mia Hammond, typed on the laptop's keyboard, entering instructions. "Just watch. The fireworks are about to start."

———

"Behold!" Bertram spread his arms, and staccato bursts of light filled the bedroom (which was really just a set, nowhere near Dalton's actual apartment). "We travel now into the *past*, to *relive* your wicked *sins!*"

The sound of thunder boomed as the lights kept flashing. Dalton sat up in bed, eyes wide, as if the booms and flashes were natural thunder and lightning, not special effects created with speakers and strobes.

"The doorway to *yesteryear* opens at my command!" shouted Bertram. Mia heard the cue in the control booth, and the wall behind him suddenly filled with the image of a spinning vortex, beamed from one of the projectors arrayed around the room. "Together, we *leap* across its threshold!" He waved for Dalton to join him.

Dalton got out of bed and staggered over in his red long johns, seemingly oblivious to the IV plugged into his right arm. The line, through which the drugs were being fed from a pump by the bed, was long enough to run the few steps to Bertram's side.

"Wow." Dalton gaped at the pinwheeling vortex. Without the LSD and sodium pentothal in his system, he would have realized the vortex was just an image projected on the white wall. No one knew *exactly* what he saw, they weren't mind-readers...but the drugs made him suggestible enough that it seemed like the real thing to him, or close enough.

"Hold on! We're passing through temporal turbulence!" Bertram reached over and gently rocked Dalton by the shoulder. Keeping the subject dialed in and distracted from any flickers of doubt was all part of the job.

Bertram felt no guilt about the trickery, either. Not after all the horrible things Dalton had done...which of course was the reason he was here in the first place.

"So…dizzy." Dalton teetered. Though he held out his arms to steady himself, he stumbled anyway and nearly fell.

Bertram caught him by the shoulder and kept him on his feet. Even with gloves on, touching Dalton made him cringe, but he knew there'd be plenty of just desserts later on to make up for it.

He would do whatever it took to get this monster to the finish line of the exercise.

"Calm yourself!" Bertram let go just long enough to clap his hands, knowing Mia would get the signal. Sure enough, the spinning vortex vanished, and footage of a verdant forest in summer appeared, expanding to cover all four walls of the room. "We have arrived! The world of two years ago surrounds us!"

Dalton wobbled as he looked around with glazed eyes and an awestruck expression. "Two…*years*…ago?" His voice was hushed. "I can't…*believe* it!"

Bertram reached back, grabbing a branch covered in leaves from a prop table. "We walk now through a leafy glade." He fluttered the branch in front of Dalton, then dragged it slowly over his head. "Do you recognize this place?"

Dalton ducked as if walking through low-hanging tree branches in a forest. "No, I don't."

"It is but a placid interlude on the way to a place you might find more familiar." Bertram raised the branch overhead and shook it, another signal to Mia. The scene on the walls changed instantly. "How about now?"

Instead of a wooded glade in the summer sun, a gruesome view surrounded them—the blood-soaked interior of a home after a brutal set of killings. It was hard to tell how many bodies there were, since hacked-up bits of them were scattered throughout the rooms in the photos...but Bertram knew.

And so did Dalton.

"Well?" Bertram gave Dalton's shoulder a squeeze. "This should be *very* familiar to you."

Dalton's mouth fell open, but he didn't say a word. He was mesmerized, gaping at one image, then another, then another.

"There's no need to be modest, Mr. Dalton," said Bertram. "Obviously, this is an absolute *work of art*. You must be so *proud*."

"The Wuh— The Wuh—" Dalton sounded as if he were stuttering. "The Way—"

"The *Waverlys*, yes." Bertram squeezed his shoulder again. "Three generations in one house. Newlyweds, bride's parents, bride's grandparents. Quite an exhibition, wouldn't you say?"

Dalton didn't answer.

"You're let down, aren't you?" Bertram clucked in mock disappointment. "No doubt, you wish I'd brought you to the peak of the action, a few hours earlier. To appreciate your artful technique in full flush?"

Dalton grunted and shook his head.

"Or perhaps..." Bertram leaned in, hooked a leather-gloved finger under Dalton's chin, and tipped his head back to stare more deeply into his eyes. "Perhaps it's the pang of *regret* that you're feeling."

———

CH-CHAK

Back in the control room, Newton shoved an ammo clip into a 9-mil pistol, then pointed it over Mia's shoulder at the laptop screen. Dalton was in his sights...Dalton's image, that is.

"Cut it out," hissed Mia. "Shoot me in the head, and I will haunt you *for real*."

"Just getting ready for go-time." Newton checked the safety and lowered the weapon. "Making sure Plan B is ready." Turning, he put the 9 down on a table alongside three other handguns. "And Plans C and D and E, as well."

"Just cool your jets," said Mia. "We need to let this play out a while longer. You, of all people, know how it works."

Of course he did. Newton was the one who'd started the group in the first place, years ago—though you couldn't blame him for being impatient today.

The team he'd assembled had made it their mission to get justice when no one else could, rooting out the darkest at-large psychopaths and making them pay in ways that fit their crimes. Four experts had joined forces—Newton the ex-cop, Mia the tech wizard, Bert the performer...and one other. One who had been the unquestioned heart and soul of the team.

Now that Amy Quinn was gone, there were only three of them. That was why today mattered so much.

"You know what's sad?" Newton picked up an insulated metal cup of coffee from the gun table and gestured at the video of Dalton and Bertram with it. "*This* is what I want for Christmas this year. *Payback*."

"Don't feel bad," said Mia. "You *know* that's not unusual."

She looked back over her shoulder at him, her emerald eyes wide behind her glasses. "Pretty sure it's at the top of *lots* of folks' Christmas wish lists."

Newton sipped the coffee and thought about how he'd just lied to her. What he wanted more than *anything*, honestly, was to have Amy alive again. In fact, if an actual demon ever popped up and made him an offer to that effect, he knew he'd jump at it in a hot second, whatever the price might be.

Maybe then, the guilty feelings would end. Maybe then, he could stop thinking about how he'd suggested he and Amy split up to cover more ground faster when investigating Dalton's latest murder scene. As tough and competent as Amy had been, she had still ended up becoming the killer's latest victim.

A victim who had been not just the heart of the team, but had broken some hearts there, as well. She and Newton had been lovers at the end, forging a relationship he'd dared to think would last a lifetime.

He hadn't been her only romance on the team, either. Amy and Bertram had also been involved a while back. Fortunately, the breakup had been clean, with no signs of open conflict or tension in the aftermath. Professional to the end, she had always made sure her personal life didn't interfere with her work.

"Here we go." Mia's fingers flew over the keyboard. "Bert just gave the signal. Time to roll out the sob stories."

"Do it," said Newton. "Shove some of that Christmas Future shit down that asshole's throat."

"That's the spirit." Mia typed some more, then decisively punched the Enter key. "You're a real Santa's elf, aren't you?"

———

"**B**e afraid!" snapped Bertram. "They are here! *The dead have come to tell their tales!*"

Dalton was visibly shivering. "The *dead? Which* dead?"

Bertram shook the leafy branch overhead. Suddenly, the image of an elderly woman appeared, superimposed over the gruesome murder scene projected on the wall. She was thin, with a neatly-styled cap of gray hair, and wore a white cardigan sweater over a top with a multicolored abstract print.

"Look!" Bertram pressed Dalton forward, closer to the photo. "It is *Claudia Palmer*, one of the victims of the massacre you committed! And she is coming closer!"

Dalton tried to back up, but Bertram kept a hand on his shoulder and wouldn't let him budge.

"She speaks!" shouted Bertram, shaking the branch again. "Claudia Palmer speaks from beyond the grave!"

Mia's voice came over the speakers in the bedroom, then. *"You ended my life in agony!"* Her voice shook like that of an old woman as she read from the script Bertram had written. Electronic distortion and reverb applied in the control room made her sound even more ghostly. *"The suffering was unbearable."*

Dalton gaped, his attention focused solely on Claudia's photo. Bertram thought he looked utterly captivated, convinced that Claudia's ghost was indeed right there, speaking to him from the afterworld.

"How could you do this to me? To my family?" Mia continued. *"Someone like you does not deserve to live!"*

Bertram shook the branch again, and the photo on the wall

changed to that of a man in his fifties—heavyset, with bushy salt-and-pepper hair and a matching goatee. He wore a red-and-green Christmas sweater with Rudolph the Reindeer's red-nosed face on the chest.

"Mr. Dalton, look!" said Bertram. "It's Claudia's son, Barry! He, too, has come to visit you at the scene of his murder!"

Again, Dalton tried to step back, and Bertram held him in place.

"You sick bastard!" This time, the voice over the speakers was Newton's, amplified and distorted to evoke a ghostly Barry Palmer. *"You made me watch as you slaughtered my loved ones, and then you ripped my guts out!"*

"Oh my God." Dalton's voice was a whisper.

Sensing they were making an impact, Bertram hiked a leather-gloved thumb in the air, requesting more effects. Mia got the message and pumped in more fog and sulfur smell, then started flashing some of the computer-controlled multi-colored lights positioned throughout the room.

"You chopped us all to pieces," said Newton as Barry. *"Made sure we felt every ounce of pain as you hacked us up and splattered our blood all over the house."*

Dalton shook his head slowly, looking shellshocked.

"You can never be absolved of sins like these," said Newton. *"But there is a way to put our spirits to rest. You can do that, at least, if you feel the slightest bit sorry."*

The lights kept flashing, the fog kept swirling. Dalton mumbled and wobbled.

"Don't you want to know what you can do to lay our spirits to rest?"

Bertram waved the branch, and a photo of all six victims appeared, superimposed over the image of the blood-soaked murder scene.

"Don't you want to do one decent thing in your misbegotten life?" asked Newton.

Dalton said nothing. He looked like he'd already checked out.

The lights flashed faster. The sound of rushing wind played over the speakers, howling like a living thing.

Bertram shook Dalton, but there was no reaction. Had the drug dosage been too strong? Had he gone into a catatonic state?

Bertram raised an index finger high, requesting a pause in the action. Then, he leaned close to Dalton and spoke directly in his ear. Maybe he could still snap him out of it.

"Mr. Dalton, it's Bertram the Christmas Demon," he said. "I'm going to tell you *exactly* what you can do to put the spirits of these victims to rest."

If Dalton heard, he gave no sign of it.

"What you can do is this," said Bertram. "You can *kill* yourself tonight, on Christmas Eve."

"Stay on script!" Newton shouted into the smaller of two mics on the control room table, the direct line to Bertram's IFB earpiece. *"No jumping ahead!"*

Bertram looked so calm on the laptop screen, it was like no one was yelling in his ear at that very moment.

"Damnit!" Newton nearly slammed his hand on the table,

then caught himself. The control room was soundproofed, but he still didn't want to take a chance that the noise might be heard in the bedroom set next-door. "This is the same kind of *bullshit* that blew it for us *last* time!"

"Calm down." Mia knew he was right about last time, but she didn't agree about tonight. "He's doing the right thing. He has to shock Dalton back into the game."

"He wouldn't *need* to if he'd been *handling* him better!"

"Hey!" snapped Mia. "Bert's doing his best! Dealing with Amy's murderer is killing him too, you know!"

Newton scowled and said nothing.

"And you do realize Dalton might have O.D.'d, don't you?" snapped Mia. "We tried to dose him just right, but..."

"But *Amy* was the *medical* expert, I know! You don't have to *remind* me!" Newton jumped off the stool where he'd been sitting, nearly knocking it over, then paced the cramped room, supremely frustrated.

Finally, he stormed over and went for the IFB mic. "I'm shutting this shit-show down."

Mia flung a hand over and blocked him from hitting the button to open the channel. "Wait! Give him a little longer! Let's see what happens!"

"I'm sick of looking at that psychopath's face. I'm sick of *all* of it. The elaborate fucking schemes to get the monsters to do themselves in when we can get the *same* result by killing them ourselves right out of the gate. Who *gives* a shit about poetic justice? Who *cares* if we avoid getting blood on our hands? Why *bother?*"

"Why bother?" Narrowing her eyes, Mia leaned closer to the laptop screen. "Because I *swear* I just saw the bastard *twitch.*"

———

"**R**emember when I told you I've come to help you see the light? Well, this is what I meant." Bertram gave Dalton's shoulder a hard squeeze, hoping to jar him from his trancelike state. "I'm here to help you see that *killing yourself* is the finest thing you can do after the kind of life *you've* lived."

Something caught Bertram's eye: a flicker of movement from the murderer? In the flashing lights and fog, it was hard to tell.

So he went on with his sales pitch, hoping he'd done the right thing—Newton's shouts in his earpiece to the contrary—in hitting the key elements sooner than planned.

"Do you know why suicide is your best option?" explained Bertram. "For one thing, you won't have to listen to the *bitching* of your victims' *ghosts* ever again. Won't *that* be nice?

"Killing yourself is also smart because it will speed your way to *Hell*...which to someone like you, will be *paradise*. You enjoy torturing and slaughtering people so much? In Hell, you can make it your *full-time profession*. With *benefits*.

"Not bad, right?" Bertram squeezed Dalton's shoulder for emphasis. "And in case you're wondering what's in it for *me*, why I'm trying so hard to *sell* you on this...listen up. There's a saying where I come from: Every time a *suicide* swings, a *demon* gets his *wings*.

"Quite simply, if I convince you to commit suicide, I get my demon wings. No more humping around the blistering waste-lands of Hell on foot!"

Bertram paused, staring hard at Dalton's face. Finally, he saw the slightest movement of Dalton's lips, as if he were speaking, though he heard no sound coming out.

Leaning closer, he pushed one ear toward Dalton's mouth, straining to hear.

"No idea. No idea." Was that what Dalton was saying? The words were so faint, Bertram couldn't be sure.

"I can barely hear you," said Bertram. "Speak up."

Suddenly, Dalton's voice got so loud that it startled Bertram, and he ducked away. "I *said*, I had no idea how *successful* I really am." Still trailing his IV line, Dalton waved at the photo of the murdered Waverly family projected on the wall. "Thank you, my friends, for *being there* for me when I *needed* you. For letting me turn you into a true *work of art*.

"You've reminded me that my life truly *is* wonderful!"

———

The control room was so quiet, Mia could hear Newton growling.

After hearing what Dalton had just said, he was literally growling in his throat. It was an ominous sound, one she'd never heard from him before. It was a sound a wild creature might make right before it went apeshit.

She was almost afraid to say a word, as if that pent-up fury might somehow be turned against her...but somebody had to say something eventually.

"This guy's a real piece of work," she said. "Even drugged and in a deep hypnotic state, he doesn't seem to experience regret. He's actually *proud* of what he's done."

Newton stopped growling but didn't answer. He just stood there, glowering at the laptop screen.

Mia sipped warm water from a bottle, considering the situation. "I wonder if we did too good a job invoking *It's A*

Wonderful Life? Maybe Dalton identifies too strongly with George Bailey. He could be acting out the wrong message from the movie, adopting life-affirming acceptance of what he's done instead of suicidal regret."

Finally, Newton spoke. "Or maybe, with someone like that, the only way to put him down is with your own two hands."

Mia swallowed hard. She didn't like hearing him talk that way. The work they did was dark, and her conscience wasn't clear—but until now, they'd always kept their feelings out of it.

They'd never had a subject who'd murdered a teammate before, though. A storm from within might be coming whether they liked it or not, a storm that could not be avoided.

Though maybe she could delay it a little longer.

"Maybe that cold-blooded prick will still come around." She reached for the remote that controlled the drug pump. "I'll boost the drip slightly—not enough to kill him, I hope— and tell Bert to keep working. Let's let this play out a bit longer…at least until we get to Amy.

"Maybe, the fresher the memories, the better chance we'll have of evoking empathy," she said, "and *breaking* the son of a bitch."

———

"Look here, Mr. Dalton." Bertram pointed at the wall, where the images of the Waverlys and their murder scene had been replaced by the spinning vortex. "We are passing through time again—moving forward into the future."

216

Dalton looked woozier as Mia boosted the drug dosage through his IV. "Bye, Waverlys." He waved lazily, eyes glazing over more than ever. "Thanks for the memories, you guys."

Bertram drew a deep breath and let it out slowly, repulsed by Dalton's flippant callousness toward his victims. It was one thing to be aware of the man's psychopathy, even to expect it—and quite another to witness it firsthand at such close proximity.

Still, he couldn't afford to dwell on that just now. It was critical that he lock away his disgust and prepare for the next performance. Somehow, he and the others had to reel Dalton back in and get him thinking about suicide instead of reveling in his horrific deeds.

A twinge of self-doubt still flickered in Bertram's heart, though, reminding him of his failure last time around. While working on another murderous subject, he'd said the wrong thing, and the subject had flown off the handle. By the time Newton and Amy had charged in to the rescue—Newton applying a sleeper hold, Amy a syringe full of tranquilizers— the subject had beaten Bertram half to death.

It was a failure he never wished to repeat...though he did feel like things might be on the verge of going sideways with Dalton right now.

"Behold!" he said dramatically. "We now emerge *one year later*, and many miles distant!"

As he said it, the vortex faded, replaced by a view of a murder scene at least as gruesome as the first. This one was also set inside a home, with hacked-up chunks of indeterminate victims scattered among slashed and gore-splattered furnishings. Strips of flesh and shreds of bloodstained clothing decorated ceiling fans and light fixtures, adding to the vision of a hellish exhibition.

"Another catalogue of atrocities," said Bertram. "All wrought by *your* fiendish hands. Three elderly sisters, all spinsters, *brutally* butchered in their own home."

Dalton's eyes widened. He took a step forward with one hand outstretched, as if he were trying to touch the carnage.

Bertram grabbed his wrist and held it fast. "But wait! The *dead* are coming to tell their *stories!* They refuse to remain *silent* a moment more!"

As he said it, a photo of a woman in her 70s or 80s appeared, superimposed over the murder scene. She wore a frizzy puff of gray hair, an olive drab dress, and glasses with tortoiseshell frames.

"The first of the dead demands to speak!" said Bertram. "*Sybil Anderson*, whom you murdered in this very place, is among us!"

Bertram waved the branch, cuing Mia. When she spoke— in a slightly lower register this time—the distortion and reverb effects again gave her voice an eerie quality.

"*Murderer!*" Her voice quavered and cracked, suggesting the cry of another elderly woman's phantom. "*How dare you come back to this nightmare you've wrought?*"

"I remember you." Dalton spoke directly to the photo on the wall. "You invited me in when I said I had car trouble."

"*And you repaid me by slashing us to pieces,*" said Mia as Sybil. "*By carving us up and desecrating our remains—even devouring some of them. All this after we welcomed you into our home and tried to help you and fed you dinner.*"

"It's true." For a moment, Dalton looked deadly serious, perhaps even apologetic...but then his expression twisted into a smirk. "Human flesh really *does* taste like *chicken*, you know."

Bertram looked at him, wondering if he was back to rejoicing in his crimes again.

"There can be no redemption for what you did to us, you maniac," said Mia. *"The best you can hope for is to lay our spirits to rest by* killing *yourself."*

Dalton's expression turned grim. "Kill myself?" A cruel smile crawled over his bearded face. "Why do that when I'm enjoying this trip down memory lane so much?"

———————

M ia clicked off the mic she'd been speaking into, pushed aside the typed script of her role, and sighed. "So much for the ghost of Sybil." Her eyes roamed to the laptop screen, watching the latest interaction between Bertram and Dalton. "But Bert still isn't giving up. He's moving on to the last scene."

"The one with Amy." As Newton said it, he reached for one of the guns. "As if it makes any difference."

"Well, he's not calling for a wrap yet," said Mia. "He must think he can still make it happen."

"I don't really give a shit *what* he thinks." Newton stuffed a gun between the waist of his jeans and the small of his back, then reached for another. "Even a moron could see he's screwed the pooch in there."

Mia whirled on him. "Do *not* go in there yet! He deserves more time! He deserves to do everything he can in memory of her!"

Newton checked the clip on the second gun, shoved it into

the front waist of his jeans, and reached for a third. "Five minutes," he said, and then he went back to growling.

"Look, Mr. Dalton. We are traveling forward again." As the image of the vortex spun on the wall, Bertram's hands shook in their black leather gloves. Adrenaline blazed in his blood vessels, galvanizing him in the lead-up to the final stage of the performance.

Dalton was chuckling, giving him no reason to think a breakthrough was possible. Even dosed to the gills on LSD and sodium pentothal, the son of a bitch was still self-possessed enough not to let a "Christmas demon" talk him into suicide.

"We have arrived!" Bertram shook the branch, and more fog poured into the room. The lights flashed faster, and the vortex disappeared from the wall. "Welcome to the world of two weeks ago!"

Dalton smirked. "Oh, good! Does this mean I get to kill that married couple again?"

"This is after that. A woman is investigating those killings, and she has found your lair." Bertram steeled himself for what was coming next. He knew he had to be strong to get through it. *There she is!*

A photo of Amy appeared on the wall before them—red-haired, smiling, in a shimmering green dress, and full of life.

"She speaks from the other side!" Bertram fought to keep up the act and keep his voice from breaking. *"She calls to her murderer! She calls to you!"*

Dalton giggled, then fell silent. He planted his glassy stare on that image and froze, his thoughts in some unreachable fugue state.

Bertram shook the branch, then shook it again. The place was filled with fog, more fog than ever, and the lights were flashing so fast, they created a strobe effect.

This time, the performance was all up to him. The team had rehearsed it with Mia playing Amy, as she'd done for the other female victims—but she hadn't been able to get through the scene, no matter how many times she'd tried. Coming so soon after Amy's death, it had been too painful for her.

Instead, Bertram had volunteered to execute this final and all-important scene on his own. He'd rewritten the script, taking it in a different direction...and the rest of the team had approved the changes. They'd agreed it had as much of a chance of working as the original approach.

But would it work as well after the final revisions he'd *secretly* made? The twists he'd incorporated without his teammates' approval? Bertram had high hopes. He thought it was probably the best thing he'd ever written.

Now was the time to put his inspiration to the test.

Leaning close, he spoke directly in Dalton's ear. "Do you know what she would ask of you, if she could?" He pointed at Amy's mist-shrouded photo on the wall. "Do you know what she would tell you to do after what you did to her?"

Dalton shook his head.

"*Nothing*," Bertram said in a hiss. "Beautiful soul that she was, she would ask *nothing* of you."

"Nothing?" said Dalton.

"But she's not here," said Bertram. "Her tortured soul is too *damaged* to cross the veil."

Without warning, Dalton flung an arm around Bertram's

shoulders and bared his teeth in a vicious glare…the look of a madman peering out from behind the drugged haze. Leaning close, he spoke into Bertram's ear. "Too bad for her, right?"

Bertram's eyes widened. "What are you *doing*, you maniac?"

"What do *you* care?" asked Dalton with a giggle.

And that was when everything changed.

———

"**W**hat the fuck?" Mia shot forward, squinting at the roiling mist on the laptop screen. "They're gone!"

"Gone where?" snapped Newton.

"I don't know! There's too much *fog* in there! They just *dropped*, and now I can't *see* them!"

Heart pounding, teeth clenched, Newton whipped open the door and charged into the hallway. He had a gun in one hand, plus two stuffed in the waist of his jeans, plus multiple clips shoved into his pockets.

He had a good idea of what he'd be facing in the bedroom, and he was ready for it. That bastard Dalton may have beaten the brainwashing and overpowered Bertram, but there was no way in *hell* he would walk away unscathed.

The bedroom door was just a few yards away, and he got there fast. It had been locked from the outside to keep the killer from escaping.

It took precious seconds to enter the code on the keypad beside the door—and then he had to do it again because he'd fumbled a digit. The second he heard the bolt disengage, he cranked the handle and flung open the door, his 9-mil raised at the ready.

At first, he saw nothing but fog churning in the doorway, flashing with intermittent bursts of multicolored light. He smelled sulfur and heard scuffling sounds in the room, but no voices.

"Dalton!" He held the gun out in front of him, hands clenched around the grip. "Get out here *now!*"

More scuffling sounds. Still, nothing visible in the fog.

Leaving the door locked and waiting it out might have been the smartest play…pumping out the fog to expose Dalton and his latest victim, then moving in hard and putting him down. But that might have meant sacrificing Bertram—and for now, there was still a chance he might be alive. As much as Bertram annoyed him, Newton couldn't just give up on him.

Cursing under his breath, Newton stepped into the room, and the door fell shut behind him. Peering into the fog, he swung the gun from side to side, trying to stay sharp…meanwhile keeping as quiet as he could.

Again, he heard scuffling. From the right? The left?
Neither.

Suddenly, a dark shadow loomed dead ahead in the mist, stuttering under the strobe effect of the flashing lights. Newton swung the gun around and locked his arms, maintaining a stiff posture at point-blank range.

Then, he paused, hoping for a positive visual I.D. before he had to pull the trigger. The lights danced around the shadowy figure, never quite landing on its face.

When they finally did, he saw it was Dalton's. He also saw Dalton's hand reaching toward him, something glinting between his fingers. A weapon?

Unwilling to take a chance that it wasn't, Newton fired the 9.

The boom of the shot echoed in the room, leaving his ears ringing. So did the next shot, and the one after that, all aimed at Dalton's center mass.

Dalton should have fallen backward, propelled by the force of the rounds pumped into him. Instead, after initially recoiling from the impacts, his body lunged forward, toppling toward Newton. Caught by surprise, Newton stumbled back and fell, the pistol flying from his hands.

Dalton's dead weight landed on top of him, pinning him to the floor...but at least the killer had taken lethal hits and was no longer a threat. Newton let out a sigh of relief, glad that the goal of the mission had been achieved...though the price had been terribly high. Dalton had been moving around free, which could only mean that Bertram had already been...

"Newton?"

At the sound of Bertram's voice, Newton's head popped up from the floor, his eyes wide with surprise. "Bert?"

Another shadow moved toward him through the mist, its outlines shifting from the strobes. The shadow descended, solidifying—and Bertram's face emerged from the cloud, smiling at him.

"Don't worry," he whispered. "I've got this."

Newton frowned. "How can you still be alive?"

As he talked, Bertram leaned down and dug the glinting object from Dalton's hand. "Shh," he said quietly. "Can you hear that?"

It was only then, when Bertram's gloved hand came around in front of his face, that Newton realized something was wrong.

The object Bertram had taken from Dalton was the needle from the IV.

In the next few seconds, additional facts quickly fell into place in Newton's mind. He realized Bertram had been setting him up all along. After dropping out of sight of the camera, he must've killed Dalton, then propped him up to draw Newton's fire (ducking away during the actual gunshots). Next, with a quick, strategic shove, he'd used Dalton's bullet-riddled corpse to pin Newton to the floor.

Realizing, further, that whatever came next would not be good for him *at all*, Newton jammed his hands under Dalton's weight in a futile grab for the gun at his waist.

"I know you hear it." As he said it, Bertram suddenly drove the needle—a custom piece, specially hardened and sharpened—deep into the side of Newton's neck and ripped through the artery there. "Ding!"

Blood sprayed everywhere, and Bertram kept ripping. Newton dug unsuccessfully for the gun, almost reaching it... until Bertram crawled up on top of Dalton, preventing further progress.

"Ding!" Bertram said a second time. "Okay, I'll tell you what that means." He chuckled softly. "They have a saying for times like this. Well, *I* have a saying." He cleared his throat. "Every time a guy like *me* makes a sound like ringing a bell, a shitbag like *you* who got the woman I loved *killed* goes straight to Hell."

Out in the hallway, Mia was calling their names and pounding on the door in a panic. Newton gasped, trying and failing to cry for help; the weight of Dalton and Bertram squeezed the breath from his lungs, and his fading strength wasn't enough to force out one last shout.

Bertram leaned closer, his eyes burning with a fire that Newton hadn't noticed in them before. It had probably been there all along, but he hadn't seen it. He hadn't realized how much the performer still cared for Amy, and how much he blamed Newton for her death.

But now he did. He realized it loud and clear and wondered how he'd ever missed it in the first place.

The clues had been there, and he'd ignored them. The clues to his own murder.

Some investigator.

"This will look like you and Dalton killed each other, though I tried to save you," explained Bertram. "Mia won't see the truth, she's no CSI...and my acting skills will further pull the wool over her eyes." His words came through faintly as the last drops of life poured out of Newton. "You'll be happy to know I'll be in the clear. And I won't lose a moment of sleep over this. You and Dalton deserve what you get."

As Bertram spoke, he heard a sequence of beeps as Mia typed in the passcode on the keypad—then did it again. Like Newton, she'd gotten it wrong the first time.

Finally, the door slammed open, and Mia charged into the room. The fog was thinning—she may have started pumping it out before running from the control room—and she saw them on the floor right away. "Newton! Bertram! Oh my God!"

By then, Newton was gone, his last breath expired. Whatever followed, it no longer mattered to him.

Bertram stood over the bodies on the floor, soaked with blood, and shook his head slowly. "Everything went so wrong." Tears rolled from his eyes. "So terribly, terribly wrong."

Mia rushed over and threw her arms around him. "This

is...this is so awful..." She held him tight as they wept and the lights danced around them.

"I know." Bertram eked out the words between sobs. "Not much...of a Christmas...is it?"

But in his heart, which hadn't always been demonic but most certainly was now, he thought it was probably the best Christmas he'd known in a long time.

CITY OF SIN STRANGLER

DAVID H. HENDRICKSON

Full-time professional writer David H. Hendrickson has been a writer for many, many years, not only as a fiction writer, but writing thousands of sports articles. He knows writing. And he knows life.

The title of this story pretty will gives you a sense of this gripping tale.

Dave's short fiction has appeared in Best American Mystery Stories, Ellery Queen's Mystery Magazine, Heart's Kiss, *and numerous anthologies, including over a half-dozen issues of* Fiction River *and just about every issue of* Pulphouse *so far. Check it all out at http://www.hendricksonwriter.com/*

CITY OF SIN STRANGLER

DAVID H. HENDRICKSON

The talk all around the city was the death of another prostitute. It was the second in three weeks, both by strangulation, both dumped near the entrance to the train station that took people from this gray, gritty city that smelled of smoke and car exhaust into Boston and back. The talk was nowhere near as overwhelming as it got about the Patriots or the Red Sox when they were in the playoffs—that was the important stuff—but there was talk.

Prostitutes were nothing new, of course, not worthy of mention other than the recurring references in the *Daily Item*'s Police Log, descriptions that had the feel of having been cut-and-pasted from all their predecessors with only a change in name and address. This city was, after all, known as "Lynn, Lynn, City of Sin (never come out, the way you went in)." Prostitutes were to Lynn what the Red Sox was to Boston.

Murder, on the other hand, was quite another thing. Lynn was bad, but it wasn't *that* bad. Murder was the exception, typically involving the drug deals that also littered the *Item*'s Police Log, usually only a handful every year, not the rule. Murders got people talking: waiting in line for coffee at Dunkin' Donuts; ordering a roast beef sandwich with mayo and cheese at Bill & Bob's; getting their vitals and medical history checked by Nora O'Sullivan before Dr. Frede, their urologist, arrived for the exam.

Nora heard it all. The attitude seemed to be that fortunately it was just whores walking the streets, selling their souls for their next high. Not good, honest people like them. Not people who counted.

They didn't say it in so many words. They used inference and euphemisms. But the message remained the same.

Not us. Just whores.

"We're better off without that scum," Charlie McGinty said in the most outspoken commentary so far, as Nora entered his vitals on her tablet. McGinty, now eighty-six, had visibly new dentures, thick-lensed glasses, and his white hair parted neatly on the side. He'd been coming to this office for forty-three years, slightly longer than Nora had been alive, and felt that he'd long since earned the privilege of stating his view on all matters that concerned him. "That's what I say. Good riddance to 'em all. If the killer gets a third one, I'll toss him a hat for the hat trick."

Nora, barely five feet tall and stocky with straight black hair cut short, felt the already small exam room close in on her. The all-white walls, bereft of any decoration save a near-life-sized chart showing the urologic internals of a male on the right and a female on the left, inched closer. The examining table on which McGinty was perched seemed to creep closer.

Nora could smell his stale sweat, the cigarette smoke in his short-sleeved, white button-down shirt and his smoker's breath.

She just wanted to get away from this man. But she needed this job, needed it in the worst way, and she knew the walls weren't really closing in. It was just those words, that attitude. She'd been hearing it all day, and from people who should know better. So she wouldn't totally rip into him. But she had to say something.

"For some mother or father," Nora said, looking Charlie McGinty right in the eye, "that dead girl is still their baby."

Charlie McGinty's head snapped back ever so slightly, as if she'd slapped him. He blinked, surprise covering his face, as if he'd been saying the same thing all day and only now had been contradicted even in the slightest.

"Well," he said. "There is that. God have mercy on them." He nodded thoughtfully, scratched the hint of white whisker stubble on his chin, and added, "Though if they'd-a brought her up right, took her to Mass every Sunday and didn't spare the rod, I bet she'd-a turned out better." He nodded in satisfaction and looked to Nora, apparently expecting a nod of agreement back.

Nora felt like volunteering to give Charlie McGinty his prostate exam herself, only with her whole damned fist, but just smiled weakly and told him the doctor would be in shortly.

As she shut the door softly behind her, her anger turned to tears. She ducked inside another exam room, still empty, before anyone could see. Only Dr. Frede himself knew, and she was damned if any of the others were going to find out.

There, but for the grace of God, go I, she thought. Not herself, of course. But Shannon, her twenty-one-year-old daughter, serving time now in MCI Framingham for a laundry list of offenses consisting primarily of drugs, prostitution, drugs, theft, and drugs. Not to mention skipping bail after Nora had scraped together every last cent of it, borrowing a good chunk, in fact, with no idea of how she'd pay it back.

Shannon. Every bit without value, in the eyes of most, as those two dead girls.

After Shannon skipped bail, Nora had sworn she was done with that girl. Finished. Kaput. But how did Nora spend a part of every weekend? Driving out to Framingham to see her daughter. What else could she do? She was Shannon's mother.

And when Shannon said, "Ma, I'm so sorry," Nora bought it. Knew it was genuine and from the heart, from one broken heart to another. Nora bought it even though she knew her girl —who had once had all the same dreams and ambitions as those who now verbally spat on her from their mighty, high horses—would almost certainly destroy herself again as soon as she got out. The hooks were in too deep. She'd stay clean for a while, but then her always-tenuous grip would slip, and she'd be back in the life.

Nora hoped to God that wasn't true, and had spent hours upon hours on her knees begging for another ending, but after a while, you just got so beaten down, it was hard to believe anymore.

Nora loved her daughter with all her heart. But Nora was so totally beaten down, she couldn't believe.

Wanted to. But couldn't.

Nora lugged the two bags of groceries up the winding, creaking, wooden steps to her third-floor apartment, wearily wondering how much new brakes would cost on the rusted-out, seventeen-year-old Hyundai she'd just left behind. The bucket of bolts had over 220,000 miles on it with tires so bald they'd never pass inspection this fall, much less be anything less than a death trap when snow hit in December. The engine went through oil so fast Nora had to top it off every week, and now the brakes were starting to grind. If it wasn't just the pads but the rotors, too, she didn't know how she'd pay for it.

They'd never been rich, but had managed to make ends meet and then a little some, their little family of four, until Mark left, deciding he'd met "the love of his life," talking as if sixteen years of marriage to Nora had been a goddamned prison sentence and Cindie, her younger, *far* more curvaceous replacement, made him feel alive again. Since the divorce almost six years ago, he'd complained almost nonstop about how he was always broke because of having to send Nora his hard-earned money, but the fact was they both were broke.

Of course, it didn't help that Josh, her fifteen-year-old son, was growing like a weed, almost six feet tall now, towering over her, always needing new clothes, new shoes and sneakers, new everything. And he had the metabolism of a furnace, able to eat three times what she ate and remain rail thin while no matter how she tried, Nora couldn't get rid of the pounds that had apparently made her so unattractive to Mark that he had to look elsewhere.

Josh, like all teenagers, burned through her money. But

Nora begrudged him nothing. He was her pride and joy. All she had left, if truth be told. Almost straight A's, and never gave her even a hint of trouble. Made his bed every day. Kept his room clean. Helped out with chores without being asked, sometimes even making dinner.

"Yes, Mom."

"Sure."

"Okay, not a problem."

Those were his responses to almost any request. Nora could never say so out loud, but he was everything that Shannon was not. Sometimes she wondered how the two could come from the same genetic material and the same environment, yet turn out so different. If Josh ever got into trouble with drugs and turned out like Shannon, it would break her heart. The very thought chilled her to the marrow. It wasn't too late for that to happen. In fact, fifteen years old was pretty close to the bull's-eye. Dear God, please don't let him turn out like Shannon.

Nora shuddered, put the two grocery bags on the dark wooden stand by the door, and fished her keys out of her purse. She unlocked the door to the apartment, carried the bags inside, toed the door shut and walked through the front room, past Josh's closed bedroom door, and into the kitchen.

"How about cheeseburgers for dinner?" she called out. Most nights, she tried to be a bit healthier than that, but tonight she was just too damned tired.

"Sure," Josh yelled back.

Nora smiled and felt just a little less weary. "How many?"

"Three? Is that okay?"

And that was the thing of it. Josh didn't *want* to be expensive. He *asked* if three cheeseburgers was okay, *asked* if something other than the absolute cheapest jeans on the market would be okay, never demanded or grew sullen if the answer was no.

Minutes later as the cheeseburgers sizzled on the grill and Nora washed the lettuce and tomatoes in the sink, Josh appeared in the kitchen, wearing a black T-shirt, jeans, and white socks with no sneakers. Towering over her, he gave her a one-armed hug.

Nora stiffened and her eyes grew wide.

"What's that smell?" she demanded.

"I farted?" he said with a grin.

"Seriously!"

"You farted?"

"What's that smell on your clothes?" Nora yelled, her heart hammering in her chest like a drum. "Don't tell me, don't tell me, don't tell me."

Josh lifted the front of his T-shirt with his thumb and forefinger and took a whiff.

"Mom, a couple of guys on the bus were smoking weed. Not me. You need to chill out." He rested a hand on her shaking shoulder, bent over and kissed her on the top of the head.

"Do you swear it?"

"I told you, it wasn't me."

"Because if you turn out like—"

Nora stopped, but the words had come out and now that they were out there, they couldn't be recalled.

Now it was Josh who was angry. "How can you even *say* that?"

"I just—"

"I hate her! I hate what she's done to you!"

"I'm fine," Nora said, shaking her head. "Really, I'm fine. I was just scared that—"

"Do you *really* think I'm so stupid that after how she turned out I'd mess with that *shit*?" He stopped as both their eyes widened at his unexpected use of *that* word. "Give me a little more credit than that."

"Okay, okay. You're right!"

"Don't *ever* compare me to her!" he yelled.

And with that, Josh stormed out of the kitchen and into his bedroom, slamming the door behind him. It was perhaps, Nora thought guiltily, the only time he'd *ever* shown anger toward her.

———

The brakes needed new pads *and* new rotors. The landlord announced another rent increase effective the month after next, then took umbrage that his advance warning wasn't sufficiently appreciated. And a third prostitute was strangled and left on a downtown sidewalk, this time outside an optometrist's office.

The talk all around the city, once muted because the death was, after all, only a whore, became almost deafening, almost on par with the Red Sox in the World Series and the Patriots in the Super Bowl. There were headlines in the *Daily Item*, and press conferences by the Police Commissioner. As with the two previous victims, there was no sign of sexual assault, and the strangulation was achieved by use of a rope. Everyone had a theory—Jack the Ripper's name was even bandied about— but almost no one *really* cared. For most, it was just a freak show, a vivid explosion of excitement to an otherwise drab existence.

And while no one at the office came close to matching Charlie McGinty's belligerent callousness—there was no talk of this third victim constituting a hat trick—Nora still had to struggle through the day, thinking of Shannon all the while, barely holding her tongue at the most ignorant comments.

"It's awful," Nora said at dinner that night with Josh, the two sitting on opposite sides of the square, wooden dining room table, a white tablecloth covering the scratches below. "Three of them."

The other night's strong words were forgotten with the sole exception of Nora knowing that she could never again compare Josh to his sister. He had even proven the unfairness of the comparison by cooking homemade lasagna with a tossed salad on the side because he'd seen her recent fatigue. It was a gesture Shannon had never made, had probably never even considered, and this was far from Josh's first time.

But it was impossible to stay away from the topic of the murders.

"I'm sorry, but those women disgust me," Josh said,

"What about the men?" Nora asked, then slid another morsel of the lasagna into her mouth, the tomato and cheese so delicious she knew she'd have to be careful or she'd devour it all night.

Josh raised an eyebrow. "The killers? Or killer?"

"No, not them. Well, of course, them. Or him. Of course, him, but I was talking about the customers. It takes two to tango. It's always the streetwalker who gets arrested—"

"Like Shannon."

"—never the customers. What about them?"

A thoughtful look crossed Josh's face as he shoveled a mouthful of lasagna in and chewed. "They disgust me, too."

Nora nodded as though she'd made a point.

"But mostly the whores," Josh said.

"Don't use that word."

"That's what they are. They disgust me." He paused as if unsure to continue. "Shannon, too. *Especially* Shannon."

"It's complicated."

"No it isn't. It's as black and white as can be."

"It's a gray world."

"You think Shannon is just a *gray* person?"

"She's a very loving girl. She just has problems."

Josh snorted. "Loving!" He shook his head in disgust.

"Yes, in her own way, she's a very loving girl."

"After what she's done to you? After what she's done to all of us? Are you serious?" Josh stared in disbelief. "I hear about her from some guys. You should hear the things they say. And I have to listen to it. About my own sister! And until she got locked up, she stole *everything*."

Nora had no answer for that.

"Remember my coin collection?" Josh asked. "Remember my full set of baseball cards from when I was seven? There were some valuable rookie cards in that collection. A signed Dustin Pedroia rookie card! All gone. She took *everything*!"

Again, Nora had no answer. The girl had taken her toll on all of them. Hell, maybe even Mark might not have looked for the "love of his life" if Shannon hadn't been making life at home so miserable.

They ate in silence for what felt like a long time, long enough at least for Josh to wolf down three helpings and her to feel frustrated that she had to stop at two.

"I'm staying over Eric's house tomorrow night, okay?" Josh asked. Eric was his best friend, also a good student and with parents that seemed nice enough.

"Yeah, sure," Nora said on autopilot, her mind stuck on Shannon's past transgressions and Josh's sweetness. "Thanks for making dinner."

"If I had less homework, I'd do it more often," he said with a smile. "But I could tell you needed it."

"Thanks, I'll clean up." Nora stood and grabbed her plate.

"No, let me," Josh said, his hand out in a stopping gesture. "Just sit on the couch and watch TV. Take it easy. Give me a holler in an hour and I'll bring you a bowl of chocolate chip ice cream."

"Oh, I've eaten more than enough," Nora said, and patted her too-ample stomach.

"You sure?"

"Oh, you know me. I'll probably holler and in less than an hour."

Josh grinned, and scooped up the plates.

"Thanks for being such a great kid," Nora said.

Josh smiled broadly. "Thanks for being such a great mom."

And as they both expected, she did give a holler half an hour later for that scoop of chocolate chip ice cream, adding "make it double."

There weren't many days that ended better.

———

A fourth prostitute was strangled and dumped on the Common down near the bandstand, and then a few weeks later, a fifth, left at the other end of the Common. Then a sixth in yet another random downtown location. And then a seventh just outside of Lynn Woods near the baseball field.

By that time, Boston-based TV news had taken notice, sending their roving reporters for live, on-site reports, and some blogger had taken to calling the killer The City of Sin Strangler, further cementing the "Lynn, Lynn, City of Sin" rhyme as the city's unfortunate call to fame. Unless, of course, the strangler would himself someday usurp that honor.

Nora didn't feel the icy fingernail of horror trace down her back until the eighth victim, a young woman whose body had not yet been discovered, a *potential* victim who was possibly not yet a victim. Nora had been tossing and turning in fits of sleep, her flannel pajamas growing damp with sweat until they clung to her skin, the darkness broken only by the red block numbers that read *3:13* on the clock radio on the nightstand.

Suddenly, Nora's eyes shot open with the dawning realization. Her mouth opened wide and a silent scream of agony erupted from deep within. Her mind, usually foggy when first coming out of sleep, instead showed her everything in pristine clarity.

It couldn't be. It just was not possible. She refused to believe it.

It was just a coincidence, one she hadn't noticed until now because...well, who would have even considered it, much less believed it? Certainly not her.

This *was* Josh, after all, the best kid a mother could ever hope for. It was insanity—a sort of parental blasphemy—to even consider the possibility.

But somewhere in the deepest, darkest recesses of her mind

the tumblers had all fallen into place, and once fallen, they remained there.

The nights before all the most recent killings—God help her for even considering the possibility—were nights Josh had stayed over at Eric's house. Somehow, while she was sleeping, her nocturnal mind had done the computations, computations her daytime mind, the rational one, would not allow. She couldn't remember sleepover nights dating all the way back to the first killings months ago, but the most recent three she was certain of and she was pretty sure of the fourth. There'd been a pattern to his sleeping over—she allowed it on school nights because he was so conscientious—and that same pattern had followed the murders.

And Josh was sleeping over at Eric's house tonight.

Feeling cold sweat trickle down her back, Nora stared at the digital clock radio.

3:17

Well, if this insane hypothesis was really true—and surely, if there was a God in Heaven, it wasn't—but if it was, the poor girl, girl number eight, was most certainly already dead. The previous estimated times of death, at least those that had been announced, had always been within an hour or at most two of midnight. So for this victim, if this preposterous notion actually had any basis in reality—which was impossible—there was nothing Nora could do to help her, to reverse an abomination already performed.

Which, of course, didn't matter because it wasn't true. It couldn't be.

But if it was…what was she supposed to do?

There was no crime to stop. It was too late for that. She'd have to wait and see if an eighth body was discovered later this morning. And if it was, she'd have to confront Josh. Ask him to somehow explain this hellish coincidence. Tell him she didn't believe it, not one last bit of it, she would never, *ever* stop believing in his innocence. He was, after all, the greatest kid ever.

But if he could just provide a sliver of proof…

Of course, if all this nonsense was really true—and certainly it wasn't, it couldn't be, but if it was—and there was some chance that the girl was not yet dead but soon would be, didn't she have the obligation to contact the police so they could save the girl? Wasn't that her legal, moral, and ethical responsibility?

But the whole idea was *insane.* Her sweet son, the best kid *ever*, couldn't have done this. She couldn't contact the police with this absurd—hideous! indefensible!—idea, then if it was proven wrong—which it most certainly *had* to be!—just say oops, my mistake, with his impeccable reputation not just tarnished but *destroyed.*

He'd be humiliated, not just by the accusation that he was a serial killer, but what would be worse, infinitely worse, was that this untrue accusation *came from his own mother*!

Trembling, Nora sat back down on the bed. She stared at the bloodred numbers on the digital clock radio.

3:24

3:25

3:26

It was the longest night of her life.

The longest night became the longest day. All the local six a.m. newscasts opened with news—live from Lynn!—of an eighth prostitute, strangled and dumped downtown, this one outside a popular pizza parlor.

Nora stared at the TV screen in disbelief. Eight dead young women.

Eight. Dead. Josh.

Those three words did not belong together. The concept shouldn't compute. Couldn't compute.

But it did.

In a daze, Nora hurriedly dressed, not caring one whit if anything matched or the buttons lined up or anything—who gave a rat's ass!—and with her whole body shaking—breaking!—grabbed her keys and drove toward Eric's house, a mile and a half away but it felt like a hundred. She parked against the curb at the entrance to the dead-end street, gripping the steering wheel so hard her knuckles had turned white. The blue, split-level house with a garage and new, tan-colored shingles was a hundred yards away, the last house on the street butting up against a patch of oak trees, a rarity in this city. Nora sat wide-eyed, and waited.

When the boys finally emerged, she resisted the urge to shoot the Hyundai forward and instead approached slowly, as if *nothing* at all was wrong—nothing!—and her whole world didn't rely on what happened the next few seconds.

"Hey Josh, can you get in?" she said as soon as she pulled up alongside them, using as even a tone as she could manage. "Eric, I'll take him to school. I'd give you a lift, too, but we have a couple family things we have to discuss. Okay?"

Eric, all red hair and freckles, had looked like he was about to bolt, but Josh touched his arm, squeezed it, then calmly slid into the front seat beside her, closed the door, and said, "Sure, Mom, what's up?"

Cool as cucumber. Not a thing wrong.

Because of course, nothing *was* wrong. Jupiter had just aligned with Mars, or something like that, and there was a perfectly fine explanation for this...this most impossible of coincidences.

There had to be.

She made a U-turn, needing to get away from Eric and this house and anyone who could possibly be watching. She pulled out of the dead-end, turned right, then back into the next dead-end she could find, and up against the curb, all the while desperately trying to keep a lid on her boiling-out-of-control emotions.

"Josh," she said in a pleading tone she couldn't prevent, "could you please tell me, please just—"

She couldn't finish. The boiling-over emotions exploded, blasting the cover off, and she burst into tears, followed by spasms of wracking sobs. Sobs that shot stabbing pains into her side and chest. Wracking sobs of the darkest sorrow, unfathomably deep in its blackness.

She tried to choke back the sobs. Tried to speak. Tried to say the words she couldn't bring herself to utter.

Josh put a comforting hand on her shoulder, and for a brief moment Nora was sure there was a logical explanation. Knew there was one, and was ashamed she'd ever doubted the best kid *ever*. How could she have ever thought such a despicable thing about him?

And when the choking sobs and salty tears finally subsided, Nora dried her tears, blew her nose with a clean, folded handkerchief Josh handed her, and looked at her wonderful son, her pride and joy, and laughed at her foolishness. She'd been so silly. She'd been such a fool to even *begin* to ask.

And the best kid ever said, "Don't worry. We won't get caught."

The bottom fell out of Nora's stomach. Her head spun. She felt as though she were about to faint.

"Pull yourself together," Josh said softly, with a maturity in his voice of a man twice his age, squeezing her shoulder in a gesture that at any other time would have offered reassurance that everything would turn out right.

Nora stared into her son's eyes. Eyes she'd always thought of as soft brown. There was nothing soft about them now.

"Are you all right?" Josh asked gently, soothingly.

She nodded yes, but no, she was most definitely not all right. Had he really admitted that…no, he had to have meant something else. Admitted to playing hooky or…or getting drunk or…or something.

Even smoking pot. Or snorting cocaine. Even shooting heroin. *Anything!*

There was some explanation for this. There had to be. And afterward, Josh would say, incredulous, "You thought I meant *that?*" Because it was, of course, impossible. He'd be incredulous and then angry that she'd thought he meant *that.*

Angry and hurt and humiliated that his own mother—*she!*—had thought that he was…

He was…

Could she even say the words? Think the words?

A serial killer?

No, no, no. Josh, her sweet, loveable, considerate Josh, who made his bed and cleaned his room and cooked her lasagna and brought her a double scoop of chocolate chip ice cream on a night when she was just so damned tired she couldn't even move. He was *not* a serial killer.

"Mom," Josh said, and tilted her head so she had to look at him through her tear-filled, blurry eyes. "I'm all you've got."

Nora felt her heart spasm, as if a powerful fist had grasped hold of it and was squeezing. Squeezing the life out of her.

She couldn't breathe. Again, her head spun. She could hardly hold it up.

"Mom," Josh said as if from a great distance. "Pull yourself together. You don't want to attract attention."

Nora blinked. She jerked her head upright. Blinked some more. Rapidly, as if doing so could change the sight before her.

"I saw on the news," she said, and though it broke her heart to even say it, she still managed the one word in a disbelieving, croaking sob. "*You?*"

Josh nodded. Coolly, dispassionately. As if affirming that he'd gotten his homework done that night. Or done the dishes. Or made his bed.

"But...*why?*"

"It's a cesspool out there. Somebody has to clean it up."

"But—"

"They're like a disease."

"But for some mother, those girls are their—"

"Yeah, their Shannon."

Once again, Nora felt her head swim. She couldn't swallow. Couldn't breathe.

When she could finally speak again, Nora said, "But she's your sister."

"*Exactly!*" Josh said, his voice cold and hard as steel on a winter day. "No more Shannons."

"I'll get you counseling," Nora offered, feeling like a drowning woman grasping at anything to stay afloat. "This isn't you. I won't say a thing as long as you change. Just talk to—"

"I don't need counseling. I know what I'm doing."

"But you have such a bright future. You can be anything you want."

"*This* is what I want."

"You can't mean that."

"I do. This is my life's work."

Nora shook her head. "No, no, no."

"If I became a doctor, would you be proud of me?"

Nora shook her head in confusion at the change of topics. "Of...of course."

"Then think of me as a doctor, specializing in cancer removal."

"This can't go on."

"It *must*."

Nora couldn't think of anything to say. Couldn't think of anything to do.

"If you even think about doing something foolish, like telling *anyone*, even Dad, about this," Josh said, "just remember, I'm all you've got."

Nora nodded dumbly.

"You understand?" Josh asked.

She kept nodding.

And not knowing what else to do, she drove him to school.

Nora got through the next few days, robotically taking blood pressures and temperatures, entering the numbers on her tablet, verifying medical histories, and saying all the right things.

"Are you okay?" people would ask, and she'd say yes, she was fine, just a little tired, not sleeping well. And that much was true. She wasn't sleeping well. She was hardly sleeping at all, drifting off only to awake with a start, drenched in sweat, the nightmare still fresh and hideously vivid in her mind.

A nightmare in which Josh was strangling some poor girl, a young woman who had once been some mother's little baby, cradling her in her arms. Her pride and joy.

But Josh had wrapped that piece of rope around her throat and was pulling it tight as that poor girl's eyes bugged out.

While she, Nora, stood next to the girl.

Watching.

Doing nothing.

The only time the nightmare varied were the times the girl was Shannon.

———

They ate dinner the next Tuesday night, a nice chicken stir-fry that Josh made for them, set out on a new checkered tablecloth he'd bought over the weekend. Only the clinking of the silverware on plates broke the silence between them.

"I'm going over to Eric's," Josh announced calmly as he stood to clear the table.

Nora couldn't breathe. She looked up at her son towering over her, his face impassive.

"No," she said, the only word she could manage.

"Yes," Josh said. "I'm not asking you. I'm telling you."

Nora tried to calm the hammering inside her chest. "But why?"

"It's easier over there."

In her mind's eye, she saw the single-family split-level at the end of a dead-end street butting up against a patch of trees. She understood that part.

"But why?" she repeated, the words the same but the question different.

"Because I have to."

"You can't keep doing this."

"We've discussed this before."

"You'll get caught. You'll spend the rest of your life in jail."

"No, we won't. We're smarter than the cops." Josh looked at her for long seconds. "The only thing that could stop us is…" He shrugged. "…you. Eric wanted to kill you as soon as you found out, but I wouldn't let him." Nora swallowed hard. Josh smiled. "I told him you'd never betray me. You can't. I'm all you've got."

Nora nodded dumbly.

"But just in case," he said, "give me your cell phone."

"Why?"

"Because we have no land line, and the cell is the one thing that could get you in trouble. In some spasm of guilt, thinking you could save some poor whore before we get to her, you might call the cops, call that anonymous number they've set up just to catch the City of Sin Strangler." He laughed at the media's nickname. "You might not be able to bear the thought of letting another whore like Shannon die. Any more than you can't bear the thought of turning me in after the deed is done. So give me your cell."

Robotically, as she'd performed so many actions in the past weeks, Nora went to the bedroom, fetched her cell where it was already charging on the nightstand, and handed it over to her son.

"Don't leave this house," Josh warned. "Don't step outside this apartment's front door. Eric's worried about you. He doesn't know just how much you love me." Josh smiled with an apparent warmth that would have filled Nora's heart with happiness back before everything changed. "He might leave me on my own tonight, come back here and make sure you don't leave this place. He says he'll have to kill you if you do.

"I'd hate to see that happen," Josh continued, "most of all because I love you." Again, he smiled. "But also because it would focus attention on me, and that would be very, very bad. It would point the cops right in my direction. And from me to Eric. It's really all that has stopped him. But if you step outside, he'll have no choice."

Josh waited for a reaction and when he got none, other than what Nora supposed was her crazed, wild-eyed stare, he added, "Besides, by now, you're an accomplice. You've known and said nothing. You'd be turning yourself in along with Eric and me. Like it or not, you're part of the team."

He smiled, then headed into the kitchen and did the dishes, humming some unidentifiable tune as he worked. Washed the dishes, dried them, and put them back in the cabinets.

A good boy.

Nora remained seated at the table, frozen, staring at the checked tablecloth.

Josh came back into the room. "Gotta go, Mom. Love you."

He bent down and kissed her on the head.

"Don't go."

"Got to."

"You're all I've got."

"Then be proud. I'm cleaning the cesspool."

———

Nora kept staring at the checkerboard tablecloth long after he left, wishing it could somehow hypnotize her into a trance she never awoke from. Josh knew her all too well. Once a poor young woman was dead and nothing could bring her back to life, Nora couldn't bear to end her own son's life, too. What was to be gained by that?

He was right. He was all she had left. And nothing would bring those dead girls back.

Eight of them!

But he was also right that she couldn't bear to allow that number to grow to nine. Somewhere, that poor girl had a mother, just like Shannon had her, and Nora could not allow another one to die. No matter what it cost.

Feeling the weight of the world upon her shoulders, Nora stumbled into her bedroom and fished out an old shoe from the back of the closet. She tilted it, and out slid a black device she had hoped never to use.

Nora stared at the disposable cell phone she'd bought several days ago. Untraceable. The tool of drug dealers and crooks everywhere.

And now, a broken-hearted mother. Who would, by its use, lose the last good thing left in her life.

She'd memorized the toll-free number. Had told herself she'd never have to use it. Josh would stop. He'd listen to her. He'd always been such a good, good boy.

But no.

And so, this was it.

With hands shaking so uncontrollably she had to reenter three of the digits, Nora keyed in the numbers for the worst phone call in her life.

NEWSLETTER SIGN-UP

DEAN WESLEY SMITH

Sign up for the Dean Wesley Smith newsletter, and keep up with the latest news, releases and so much more—even the occasional giveaway.

Go to **deanwesleysmith.com.**

Sign up for the WMG Publishing newsletter, too, and get the latest news and releases from all of the WMG authors and lines, including *Pulphouse Fiction Magazine, Smith's Monthly,* and so much more.

To sign up go to **wmgpublishing.com**.

Follow Dean on BookBub

ABOUT THE EDITOR

DEAN WESLEY SMITH

Considered one of the most prolific writers working in modern fiction, with more than 30 million books sold, *USA Today* bestselling writer Dean Wesley Smith published far more than a hundred novels in forty years, and hundreds of short stories across many genres.

At the moment he produces novels in several major series, including the time travel Thunder Mountain novels set in the Old West, the galaxy-spanning Seeders Universe series, the urban fantasy Ghost of a Chance series, a superhero series starring Poker Boy, and a mystery series featuring the retired detectives of the Cold Poker Gang.

His monthly magazine, *Smith's Monthly*, which consists of only his own fiction, premiered in October 2013 and offers readers more than 70,000 words per issue, including a new and original novel every month.

During his career, Dean also wrote a couple dozen *Star Trek* novels, the only two original *Men in Black* novels, Spider-Man and X-Men novels, plus novels set in gaming and television worlds. Writing with his wife Kristine Kathryn Rusch under the name Kathryn Wesley, he wrote the novel for the NBC miniseries The Tenth Kingdom and other books for *Hallmark Hall of Fame* movies.

He wrote novels under dozens of pen names in the worlds

of comic books and movies, including novelizations of almost a dozen films, from *The Final Fantasy* to *Steel* to *Rundown.*

Dean also worked as a fiction editor off and on, starting at Pulphouse Publishing, then at *VB Tech Journal*, then Pocket Books, and now at WMG Publishing, where he and Kristine Kathryn Rusch serve as series editors for the acclaimed *Fiction River* anthology series.

For more information about Dean's books and ongoing projects, please visit his website at www.deanwesley-smith.com and sign up for his newsletter.

For more information:
www.deanwesleysmith.com

f facebook.com/deanwsmith3
P patreon.com/deanwesleysmith
BB bookbub.com/authors/dean-wesley-smith